Strings of FAITH

Praise for *Strings of Faith*

"Against the backdrop of bluegrass festivals, music, and musicians, Terry exposes the weakness of human spiritual leadership and often misguided, hurtful church traditions. Through the lives of ordinary people, he is able to show us that only strength of faith, close friends, and spiritual fellowship can keep the music alive within us. *Strings of Faith* strikes just the right chord! As a pastor of twenty-two years, I can tell you that Terry's *Peghead Solution* will tune up your spiritual life once and for all. Don't just read it….do it!"

—Don Adkins, Senior Pastor at Christ Central Church, Cocoa, Florida

"Terry Stafford fully understands the amazing power of music to heal the body, mind and spirit. It is no accident that beautifully played string music is capable of "plucking our heart strings." Whether a toe-tapping, spirit-lifting hoe-down or a tender, romantic waltz, the sounds of an old time fiddle tune can carry both player and listener to a better place. Old time fiddle music connects the years and ties generations together by a common thread. Sometimes, it is this tenuous thread that allows peace and healing. Terry takes us on a beautiful journey of music and self-discovery. I would like to think this story is in part, the story of some of the real-life competitors at the National Oldtime Fiddlers' Contest, who have had similar struggles, challenges, and experiences."

—Sandra Cooper, Executive Director National Oldtime Fiddlers Contest and Festival. Weiser, Idaho

Also by Terry Stafford

Freedom to Worship: One Church On a Journey

Strings of FAITH

BY TERRY STAFFORD

AUTHOR ACADEMY elite

Published by Author Academy Elite
P.O. Box 43, Powell, Ohio 43035

www.AuthorAcademyElite.com

Paperback ISBN-13: 978-1-943526-61-1
Hardcover ISBN-13: 978-1-943526-60-4

Library of Congress Control Number: 2016911230
Author Academy Elite, Powell, OH

Dedication

This book is dedicated to the many Christians who have been disappointed, hurt, or pushed away from the church by misguided leaders within organized religion—yet through it all, choose to remain faithful to God and the one united church that Jesus built.

Also, I dedicate these words to those who seek the salvation that only Jesus can offer, but have been hesitant to approach the church because of the unfortunate reputation we have earned. Please don't give up on us. We are all imperfect human beings. Your salvation is critical, and we want to see you *there* with us.

Finally, I dedicate this story to those who seek *joy made full*—those recovering from the seemingly endless pain and struggles of life. When you need hope, remember your dream. It was planted in you for just such a time as this. When you need faith, be thankful for the many blessings that live all around you. When you need peace, forgive those who have hurt you. Find empathy in your heart for their plight and continue to look forward. May God bless us, all.

Table of Contents

"Consult not your fears but your hopes and your dreams. Think not about your frustrations, but about your unfulfilled potential. Concern yourself not with what you tried and failed in, but with what is still possible for you to do."
~ Pope John XXIII

Foreword

I first met Terry when he joined our Author Academy Elite online group. His profile photo showed him holding a guitar, not something I see often. I thought it was cool when I learned he had been a worship leader in his church for many years and was also a bluegrass musician. But then I read some of his work and realized he followed a dream he didn't even know he had.

Too often, we allow ourselves, or others, to set our dream aside to live a socially acceptable life. We fail to recognize what was planted deep within us when we were just children. God gives us a gift in order to pursue the seed of a dream he planted in us, or even to reach that magical place just beyond the dream.

In *Strings of Faith*, Terry captures the essence of what it means to have close friends to help you find clarity and return to the path of a long-abandoned dream. While there are many novels that depict a hero's journey, and finding contentment through adversity, this story has an intriguing thread of music and culture from America's heartland. You can almost hear the music in the story.

The journey that the protagonist, Darcy, travels, is one of both pain and joy—often unexpected turns between the two. When God is leading, is it surprising that even a most ardent enemy can turn out to be your saving grace—an answer to your prayers? Take nothing or no one for granted. Brace yourself for a powerful story of tragedy, faith, and the resurrection of a dream.

Kary Oberbrunner, CEO of Igniting Souls. Co-creator of Author Academy Elite.

Introduction

Every now and then, there is a story of celebration or tragedy that lives inside a family, screaming out to be told. This story has been yelling at me for most of my adult life. The story is too painful to be told as a non-fiction account or memoir, so I have chosen to tell a true story surrounded by fictional characters based on real people in fabricated locations and circumstances. In fact, it will be nearly impossible to discern the painful truth except by those who lived it. That is by design.

In writing this book, it occurred to me that the embedded story itself isn't all that important beyond our immediate family. Those memories are real. But what is important now, is using this story to help others understand pain and tragedy, in order to build a foundation from which to climb out of the pits of anger and self-destruction. This story proves that the joy of contentment can arise from adversity.

Dr. Wayne Dyer has been quoted as saying, "Don't die with your music still within you." That was actually a paraphrased version of a quote he used by Oliver Wendell Holmes, who said: "Many people die with their music still in them. Why is this so? Too often it is because they are always getting ready to live. Before they know it, time runs out."

Enjoy the journey, for the journey inspires the music.

CHAPTER 1

Gathering

*"Then David spoke to the chiefs of the Levites to appoint their
relatives the singers, with instruments of music, harps, lyres,
loud-sounding cymbals, to raise sounds of joy."*
~ 1 Chronicles 15:16

The motorhome roared down the dirt road, traveling way too
fast to safely navigate the overhanging trees and deep pot-
holes. As Kevin came banging and crashing by Darcy's campsite, he
screamed out of the open driver's window in his loud twangy voice.

"We're heeeeere!"

Sitting on the steps of a new blue-and-white motorhome,
her long blonde hair blowing across a worn denim jacket, Darcy
returned the yell.

"Yahoooo! Let's pick!"

Doubting that Kevin heard her, Darcy lowered her arm with a
smile and went back to reading, waving the dust away from her face.

She saw Ben stirring on the cot he was laying on in front of
the motorhome. He turned to lay flat on his back and stared at the
blue sky. Ben had been a dear friend of Trevor and Darcy for many

years. He was also a very talented guitar player and member of their band. Darcy followed his gaze and looked up into the sky through the lush green leaves dancing back and forth in the breeze.

She saw Ben turn his head when they both heard the high-pitched, hollow resonance of a banjo playing in the distance, echoing across a field between the tree-lined, barbed-wire fences. They could barely hear a guitar accompanying the banjo. Voices, weak in the breeze, sang some unidentifiable but really fast song.

After lying still for a few minutes, apparently enjoying the peaceful collection of his thoughts, Ben lifted his feet and threw them off the side of the cot. He rocked up into a sitting position and rubbed his face, finally resting it in the palms of his hands. He slid his hands away and opened his eyes again to see the edge of the woods in front of him.

"What the heck was that?" Ben asked.

"It was Kevin. He finally made it." Darcy nodded at him. "Are ya nursin' a hangover?"

"Heavens no. I just haven't slept that hard in a long time."

Ben stood up, scratching his head, and turned to look toward the music. "Who's that over there pickin' so early?"

"So early?" Darcy giggled. "It's after ten o'clock, Ben."

"Well, good grief. I must have played way too late last night. Or was it this morning? How long have you guys been up?"

"We got up and out a couple hours ago. We went over to get some coffee and a bite to eat."

She looked across the field in deep concentration at the small group of musicians gathered in a circle under a tarp. Her head twisted just a little as she tried to figure out the tune.

"I think it's that bunch from Ohio," she finally answered. "Buckeye...somethin' or other."

"I heard them play a little last night," Ben said. "That guitar player is killer! I think I'll go over there and see what they're workin' on. Maybe steal a few licks."

Darcy nodded with a smile as Ben turned to head out across the field. After he was out of sight, she shifted her gaze, first to her book, then to the woods, sinking back into the daydream that had held her captive before she was interrupted by Kevin's arrival and Ben getting up. In the deep recesses of her daydream, she heard the sounds again, a cheering crowd shouting her name and applauding as she amazed them with her fiddle playing. She smiled and her eyes sparkled, enjoying the vision as she had done so many times before.

Born in Louisville to parents who were both professors at Bellarmine College, Darcy grew up with discipline, proving repeatedly that she could succeed at whatever challenge she chose to take on. When she was eleven years old, she was asked to play her violin at a founders-day event in front of the courthouse. Her father objected to it, fearing that taking the time to perform well would distract her from her schoolwork. Darcy missed supper every evening for two weeks while she practiced her violin solos, and then did her homework.

Her father finally yielded, recognizing the highly unusual self-discipline for such a young girl. Her performance at the courthouse drew a rousing response and a wonderful article in the local newspaper. As important as academic success was to her, her true love had always been her violin.

With the support and encouragement of her mother, Darcy grew in the music and perfected her mastery of the instrument. She impressed her teachers throughout her grade school years. When she played, her small hands gently cradled the neck, playing with a soulful grace that one would never expect from a child. She played with clarity and confidence, moving so swiftly that anyone watching could barely see her fingers.

When Darcy left high school, she attended her parents' alma mater, Bellarmine College, where she graduated with a degree in instrumental music. From there, she was accepted into The Boston Conservatory.

After mastering the classics, such as Bach's *Brandenburg Concerti* and Brahms's *Ein Deutsches Requiem* violin concerto, she discovered from her new friends at the Conservatory something she hadn't heard back at Bellarmine— roots music. She heard the soulful sound of bluegrass and rustic old-time music born in the Appalachian Mountains, passed down through generations of Scots-Irish and African ancestry. Her heart leapt as she heard the spirited sounds of the acoustic strumming, fiddling, singing, and dancing. She was instantly hooked.

Darcy's parents were less than pleased with her change in direction. It was difficult for them to understand why a child with such talent and investment in her craft would throw it all away for something so primitive. They no longer accepted her music choices, and it put a strain on their relationship.

As Darcy stared into the woods, still sitting on her motorhome steps at the campground, she saw herself playing and winning at The National Oldtime Fiddle Contest in Weiser, Idaho, the fiddler's granddaddy of all contests that her friends had told her about back in Boston. She smiled again and shook her head, awakening from her daydream.

"Honey, would you hand me my fiddle?" she yelled through the screen door.

Trevor Marshall, Darcy's husband of two years, handed the fiddle and the bow through the door.

"Practicing for the Nationals?" he asked with a smile.

She giggled. "How did you know that's what I was thinking about?"

"Lucky guess," he said. "Are you okay?"

"I'm fine."

"I mean about the doctor."

"I know what you mean."

"Do you want to talk about it?"

"Not really. Not right now, anyway."

"Have you seen Judy yet?" Trevor asked.

"No," Darcy said softly.

She had been thinking about Judy all day—her dearest friend in the world, even though they only saw each other a few times a year when they camped or played music together. This time, Darcy really needed to talk to her.

Trevor smiled and went back into the motorhome.

Darcy tucked the old, worn wood of the fiddle under her chin. She grasped the bow lightly with her right hand as if to caress a delicate flower. As soon as the bow touched the strings, the fiddle sang a melody in its own voice—so beautiful that the birds stopped to listen. She played the tune of a slow, droning mountain hymn, revealing her soul through sounds weeping from the instrument.

Ben, rather short and stocky, stepped high through some of the tall wiregrass, crossing the field to get to the musicians playing under the tarp at their campsite. When he arrived, he stood outside the circle of musicians, assuming that he wouldn't be noticed. He was a little startled when a voice came from the group, obviously speaking to him.

"Where's your guitar, man?"

"I left it over there at the camp. I just stopped in to listen a little," Ben said.

"I really enjoyed the jammin' last night," the man said as he stepped forward holding his guitar.

"The name's Jack, by the way. Jack Hanford."

Ben, reaching to shake Jack's hand, leaned in through the crowd of listeners. "Ben Salinger. Pleased to meet you."

"You guys playin' in the contest at Athens?" Ben asked.

"Wouldn't miss it for the world. We've won it the last three years. I see no reason to stop now," Jack said with a smirk.

Although Ben was a little taken aback by the tone of arrogance, he wasn't prepared for what came next.

"Is that little blonde fiddle player over there, with you guys?" Jack asked. He had a look of disgust on his face. Before Ben could answer, Jack continued. "I heard we had a classical violin player over there somewhere. I don't know why those people don't just keep to their own. They obviously don't have the feel to play our kind of music. They're gonna ruin it! She needs to just go back home. She'll never get on this stage here."

Ben paused in disbelief. His cheeks flushed.

"Maybe we'll see you later," Ben said, gritting his teeth, jaw bones throbbing. He turned away and left the circle, shaking his head. He couldn't get away soon enough.

Darcy had only played her fiddle for several more minutes after Ben left her campsite, before she decided to join him.

"Honey," Darcy called out to her husband. "Would you grab this fiddle? I'm gonna run over there where Ben is and see what's goin' on."

She handed Trevor the fiddle and cheerfully pranced across the field in anticipation, her bouncing golden hair glimmering in the sun behind her. She started to walk around a camper when she overheard the conversation between Ben and Jack about her classical training. She froze and listened to his attacks. Shocked and embarrassed, she ducked away behind the camper so Ben wouldn't see the angry tears welling up in her eyes.

She quickly walked back across the field to the motorhome, hoping no one saw her. Already emotionally exhausted from her visit to the doctor the week before, Darcy had a difficult time registering what she had just heard. She worked so hard to learn this music and now veterans were rejecting her.

As soon as Ben cleared the campsite, his squinted gaze dropped to the ground in front of him to avoid eye contact with anyone, his fists clenched. He continued to shake his head, seething at the thought of what Jack had just said about Darcy. She was practically his little sister.

He decided to take a walk through the vendor area to cool off. He wanted to see what everyone had to offer, knowing the same vendors peddling the same wares would be sitting in the same spots as they did every year for as long as he could remember. He walked slowly across the field toward a canopy of oak trees where trailers and tents were lined up while the masses of people that were gathered, flipped through cassette tapes and albums, tried on shirts and hats, or scouted out the latest gadget that would help an instrument play itself.

He walked under the trees, the sun in his eyes finally interrupted by the shade. Ben caught sight of a food cart with carnival art painted all over the sides and lights flashing around the top. The sign read, *FUNNEL CAKES*, one of the delights Ben looked forward to with anticipation each year at the festival.

"Ah, perfect," he muttered.

Through years of experience, he knew that eating a funnel cake would be messy. So, he decided to wait until after he'd walked the line of vendors and checked out everything else.

Back at camp, Darcy timidly played her fiddle again, her confidence shaken. Her hand shook around the fiddle's neck as she tried to lose herself in the music. Instead, she replayed in her mind again and again what she had overheard.

"How can I be ruining the music?" she thought. "My God, I'm ruining the music!"

Several strangers stopped to listen and chat but she was so consumed with her thoughts, she didn't even acknowledge them, and so they eventually continued on their way. She sat alone in front of the motorhome playing slow, lonesome tunes on her fiddle. As she pulled the bow back and forth across the shiny strings, she caught a glimpse of a shadow moving toward her. Just then, a voice rang out.

"Hey, pretty girl!"

Darcy turned with a jolt and saw the slender redhead in blue jeans coming around the motorhome.

"Judy!" Darcy screamed as she jumped up from the steps and ran to meet her friend.

Darcy threw her arms, along with a bow in one hand and a fiddle in the other, around Judy's neck, almost getting caught up in the sweater sleeves Judy had draped over her shoulders and loosely tied around her neck.

"Sorry it took me so long to get over here," Judy said. "We had some RV trouble coming around the loop."

"I am so glad to see you," Darcy said. "I've missed you so much!"

"Well, I've missed you too, sweetie. As soon as I climbed down from the RV, I heard that beautiful fiddle and knew it was you."

"Come on over here and sit. Hey, Trevor, look who's out here!" Darcy said.

"I heard, I heard," Trevor said. He opened the screen door and stepped outside. "Hey gorgeous. How are you doin', girl?"

"Doin' fine, doin' fine," she said as she walked to him.

He wrapped his muscular arms around her in his familiar bear hug.

"You girls catch up," Trevor said. "I'm gonna walk around and see if I can catch up with Ben."

He smiled, knowing Darcy had been waiting for Judy to show up so they could talk.

"Okay, hon," Darcy said. "You guys don't stay gone too long. We're gonna eat here in a bit. As soon as Kevin shows up, we'll do some pickin'."

"Sounds like a plan. I'll see you shortly."

As Trevor walked out of sight, Judy leaned in and whispered, "I swear that man of yours gets better lookin' every time I see him."

"I'm a lucky girl," Darcy said with a chuckle.

"So, what have you been up to?" Judy asked. "I can't believe it's been a year already."

Darcy was stunned by Judy's comment. It really had been that long. "I know. I've really missed you." She cleared her throat. Her excited smile quickly gave way to sadness.

"I got some awful news last week, and I've wanted to talk to you about it. I hope you don't mind me dumping this on you before you've even had time to set up camp."

Judy's smile turned to concern. "You don't think a thing about it, sweetie. Let's go inside and talk so I can get something to drink. You got some of your iced tea in there?"

"I just made a batch this morning. Come on in."

Judy followed Darcy up the steps, closing the door behind her. "I love your sweet tea," Judy said.

She sat down and leaned forward, her arms spread across the table. She looked around, examining the detail in the trim and the decorations—Darcy's handiwork.

"It's some of that good Louisville tea my mom taught me to make," Darcy said. "I know you don't like sugar, though. Sorry about that."

"Oh, no. I'm fine. I always make an exception for your iced tea. When did you guys get this big ol' motorhome? It's beautiful."

"We picked it up last fall. As much as we love going to festivals, it just made sense. We discussed it for quite a while and decided we should get one before we had kids."

Darcy's voice cracked and she paused. "Then, we would always have plenty of room for camping." Darcy dropped her head to her hands and began to sob, taking Judy by surprise.

"Oh, honey, are you okay?"

Judy leaned over the table again and put her hands on Darcy's arms.

"I'm sorry," Darcy said, wiping her hair back from her face. "I feel like I've been holding my breath since last Wednesday."

"Well, what in the world happened?" Judy asked.

Darcy pulled her hair back, tying it in a knot behind her head. She sighed and stared at her glass, dripping with condensation. She wrapped both hands around it.

"Trevor and I were beginning to get worried after two years of trying, and we weren't getting pregnant. After Christmas, we started seeing a doctor. He sent me to all kinds of specialists."

She stopped talking and looked out the window. She focused on the lake in the distance for a moment before her gaze turned back to the glass.

"Well, to make a long story short, he told me I have ovarian something-or-other syndrome. I'm infertile," she said. Her eyes filled with tears again, but she held them back.

"Oh, sweetie, I'm so sorry," Judy said. She cupped her hands over Darcy's, still holding the glass. "Is that the end of it? Isn't there anything they can do?"

"Apparently, there's nothing." Darcy sighed, pulling her hands away. She stood up and went to the refrigerator to take out the ground beef and other food to start preparing supper.

"How is Trevor handling it?" Judy asked.

"Oh, he was shocked at first, maybe disappointed. I don't know. I think he's okay now."

"You poor baby." Judy stood silently, went to the sink, and began slicing the tomatoes Darcy had taken out of the refrigerator.

Trevor caught up with Ben in the vendor area, shoving a funnel cake in his face, white powdered sugar on his nose and chin.

"Good grief, Ben!" Trevor shouted.

Ben was startled. Still holding the pastry halfway in his mouth, he jumped and turned quickly to the side to get out of the way.

"You've got that thing all over you!" Trevor said.

Ben looked at Trevor and started laughing. He doubled over with a hand over his mouth, trying not to spit everything out. Trevor couldn't help but laugh, too. "Hey man, get a grip!" he said.

People all around them were watching the calamity. Ben finally swallowed the funnel cake, coughing then laughing, then bent over on his knees, tears rolling down his face. Clouds of confectioner's sugar billowed through the coughs and laughter.

Trevor walked quickly over to the vendor's trailer. "Would you give me a cup of water, please, before this guy over here suffocates?"

The vendor smiled and quickly handed Trevor a cup of water. Ben sat down on a picnic table to catch his breath.

"Here," Trevor said, handing the paper cup to Ben. "Are you gonna make it?"

"I'm fine. You scared the bejeebers out of me, man," Ben said. He took a drink.

They both erupted, uncontrollably laughing again. Ben spit a mouth full of water into the air, missing Trevor by inches. He sprayed the entire picnic table and several feet around it.

"Come on, let's get out of here before we get arrested," Trevor said.

He grabbed Ben by the arm and pulled him up from the table. They walked across the vendor area, under the trees and into the field, laughing and trying to ignore the people looking at them.

"We need to get back to camp," Trevor said.

By the time they arrived back at camp, the hamburgers were sizzling on the grill.

"Mmm, smells good!" Ben said. He stared at the grill in anticipation.

"Good grief! You just about choked on a funnel cake, and now you're over here acting like you're starving to death." Trevor said.

They told Darcy and Judy about their escapades at the funnel cake trailer, and everyone had a good chuckle.

"Can't take you guys anywhere," Judy said. "Hey, I need to get back to my camp. I'll leave you alone to eat, and I'll catch up with you in a little bit when Kevin's ready to pick."

"Can't you stay and eat with us?" Darcy asked, with her lower lip puffed out.

"No, you guys go ahead. I've got to get my place put together before it gets too dark. Tom's going to send the dogs out after me."

"Okay. We'll be over as soon as Kevin gets set up," Darcy said.

After Judy left, Darcy began collecting the hamburgers from the grill, smoke and flames shooting up a foot above the white-hot coals.

"Trev, there's some beans and potato salad up there on the counter by the sink. Would you grab that and some pop from the cooler?"

When Trevor walked inside, he noticed the two glasses sitting on the table in a pool of water. He knew Darcy and Judy had spent some time talking. He smiled as he picked up a 2-liter bottle of pop and the two bowls from the counter. "Hey Ben, grab the door."

After all the food was spread on the table, the three sat quietly beneath the setting sun. Trevor looked across the table at Darcy, noticing her red puffy eyes, and gave her a tender smile.

"Grab a hand," Ben said, breaking the silence.

Ben said a short prayer while Trevor looked on awkwardly.

"Amen," they all said together.

After about thirty minutes, the food was gone and the conversation exhausted.

"Well, I'm gonna get this mess cleaned up," Darcy said, as she gave out a sigh. "I'm stuffed."

Ben got up from the picnic table. "If you guys don't mind," he said, "I'm gonna grab my guitar and run over to Kevin's place. He's probably set up by now. The burgers were great, Darcy, as always."

"We'll catch up in a bit," Trevor said.

Ben's guitar case had been leaning against the side of the motorhome. He picked it up and left as Trevor and Darcy carried empty dishes up the steps. They cleared the table, loaded the sink, and put leftovers in the refrigerator.

"Good stuff," Trevor said, rubbing his stomach.

"I love being out here," Darcy said. She smiled and walked across the floor and pressed against Trevor, wrapping her arms around his waist. She looked up at him with her big green eyes as he folded his arms around the back of her neck.

"I love you," Darcy said, pressing her nose into his chest.

"Are you okay?"

"I'm fine," she said.

"I take it you finally got to talk to Judy about everything."

"Yes, I did. I'm sorry, honey. Please don't be offended that I wanted to talk to her about it."

Trevor smiled. "I'm not offended at all, baby. I knew what you were waiting for."

"How are you doing, Trev?" she said in a more serious, deliberate tone.

Trevor paused for a several seconds, let out a sigh, and said, "You know, babe, I really believe we're going to get through this okay."

"Yes, God will take care of us," Darcy said.

"I suppose," he said.

"But what are we going to do now? I want to have a family with you, Trevor."

"I know, baby." Trevor paused again and gazed outside the window over the dining table. "We'll have a baby one way or another. That's a promise."

Darcy pulled back a little and looked into his eyes. He returned her stare with a smile.

"I believe you, honey," she said. She stretched up on her toes and gave him a kiss. "I believe you."

CHAPTER 2

Sharing

*"For where two or three are gathered in my name,
there am I among them."*
~ Matthew 18:20

Kevin and Judy were sitting in front of a 55-gallon drum that was glowing red from the fire inside it, when Trevor and Darcy walked up to Kevin's campsite, instrument cases in hand.

"Let's pick!" Trevor shouted as they emerged from the darkness.

Kevin saw them and screamed his normal blood curdling greeting. "Aaaaaaaeeeeeeeeeee!"

He quickly propped his standup bass against the old motorhome and ran over to the couple, embracing them in a group hug. It was a little awkward with their instrument cases, but that was nothing new.

"Man, it's great to see you guys," Kevin shouted.

Kevin was another dear friend and bass player for the band. He was from Columbus, Ohio, but pretty much called everywhere home. He traveled more than most people would ever consider, but was usually available when it came time to play music. His arrivals were always loud and obnoxious, but quite effective. He loved everyone and everyone loved him.

Both Trevor and Darcy cringed as Kevin's face was right next to their ears as he yelled, still with his arms wrapped tightly around each of their necks. "Did ya'll eat yet? I've got plenty!"

Kevin had already set up two long tables along the side of his motorhome and had all kinds of food spread along the length of them. Two pots full of chili were the main dish.

"I told you they were over there eating," Judy said.

"Yes, we just ate." Darcy pushed him away as she laughed. "I thought Ben was over here."

"He was," Judy said. "But he took off over yonder to see who's jamming where."

Trevor laid his banjo case on the picnic table. He opened up the case and gently lifted the neck of his banjo. Darcy sat on a lounge chair and laid her fiddle case across her lap. As the campfire glistened in her hair, she eased the fiddle out and hooked the chin rest on it, then laid it back in the case as she grabbed a small pouch containing a block of rosin in her left hand and took the bow out of the hooks in the top of the case in her right hand. She slid the rosin up and down the length of the horse hair as she had done all of her life to get it to vibrate the strings just right. Judy watched her every move, witnessing the preparation of a master.

"How long have you had that fiddle?" Judy asked.

"I bought it two years ago from old man Ferguson right after I left the Conservatory," Darcy said. "Man, that upset momma and daddy to no end, when I traded down from my last violin."

"Ah, Woody Ferguson," Kevin said. "He's so darn good. He has his workbench set up over there behind the funnel cake booth, as usual."

Trevor broke out laughing. Then Darcy got tickled and couldn't stop laughing.

"What?" Kevin asked. He started laughing too, even though he had no idea what he was laughing about.

Judy chimed in with a giggle. "I haven't told him about it yet."

As soon as Trevor regained his composure, he told Kevin about Ben nearly choking to death earlier that afternoon at the funnel cake booth. They all had a good laugh at Ben's expense.

"I need to go over there and see Woody," Darcy said, when she regained her composure.

"Well, let's pick first!" Kevin shouted.

By then, Trevor, who was standing next to the picnic table, had the banjo strap over his shoulder. Darcy put the rosin away and laid the case on the ground behind her chair.

"Do something easy," Judy said as she rested her mandolin up in her lap. "I know, Darcy. Do that tune, *Faded Love*. It's a good one to warm up with."

"Okay." Darcy raised the fiddle to her chin and kicked off a sweet love song based on an old fiddle tune called *Darling Nelly Gray*.

Kevin grabbed his bass and joined them. Trevor started a slow easy roll on his banjo while Judy started chunking her mandolin. Almost immediately, people began gathering around the campsite, the fire from the 55-gallon drum casting an orange glow on their smiling faces.

Many people came to the bluegrass festival just to listen and enjoy the company of musicians, but couldn't play a note themselves. There were many festivals that were just attended by musicians playing for other musicians. But this, The Festival of the Bluegrass near Lexington, wasn't one of them.

Two or three instrumental tunes went by before Ben quietly walked in and worked his way through the crowd. He took his guitar out of its case and joined in. The rhythm made all the difference in the world. After a couple more tunes, Darcy interrupted. "Where have you been, son?"

"I was over there listening to Jack and those guys."

"What do ya think?" Trevor asked.

"I think we can take 'em."

"I am so looking forward to that," Darcy said.

"Hey Judy, can you play with us down at Athens in October?"

"In Alabama?"

"Yeah, it's the fiddler's convention down there at Athens State College. They have a bluegrass band competition in the middle of all the old-time fiddlers."

"Sure! Sounds like fun."

They jammed around, playing and singing for a couple of hours before Judy said, "Hey guys, I'm beat from that drive today. I think I'm going to turn in."

"I think we are too," Trevor said.

Everyone said goodnight and Kevin took his bass back into his motorhome before he and Ben walked into the darkness, guitar cases in hand, making their way around the park to join in the jamming. There were campfires sparkling through the trees as far as the eye could see in any direction. The symphony of musicians echoed throughout the park, different instruments accompanying a variety of songs in different keys, at different tempos. It was a unique chaos, and a somewhat soothing sound to the avid bluegrass festival goer.

Kevin and Ben walked slowly past each jam circle, noticing the size of the listening crowd to see how it was going. There always seemed to be too many banjo players or too many guitar players or too many bass players or too many mandolin players. If they walked up on just the right group, they would ask whoever seemed like they were heading things up, if they could join in. It was merely a formality since nobody ever said no. Most everyone knew each other, at least among the musicians.

The two ended up at the camp next to Woody Ferguson's booth, where he built and repaired acoustic musical instruments. Woody wasn't working but was there in the corner, just out of the way, his long white beard glowing in the light of the fire, his wire-rimmed glasses hiding his eyes behind the reflection of the flames.

"Hey Woody!" Ben said. "How's it going?"

"Doin' real good, Ben. Doin' real good. How's that neck a holdin' up?"

"Oh real fine, sir. Like it never happened."

The year before, Ben had left his old Martin guitar leaning against a picnic table when somebody fell against it and cracked the neck. Ben was devastated but remained cool as the perpetrator apologized profusely. Woody was able to repair the damage almost to perfection.

"Man, that was awful," Kevin said. "Hey Woody, Trevor and Darcy are here, and Darcy wants to see you. They've turned in for the night, but she'll probably be over here looking for you in the morning."

"Well, I'll be right here. Is she okay?"

"I think so," Ben said. "I can't put a finger on it, but she does seem a little off this trip."

"She's a sweet, sweet girl, that one is," Woody said. "She plays that fiddle like no one I've ever heard."

"Yeah, we're blessed to call them friends," Kevin said.

"Hey! Break 'em out, boys," yelled a voice from the other side of the fire.

Ben squinted his eyes to see through the flames, and smiled when he saw who it was.

"Doc! Man, how are you doin'?"

Doctor Josh Packard walked around the fire and through the crowd with his banjo hanging from his shoulder to get to Ben and Kevin. Dr. Packard, or Doc, as his friends called him, was a sociology professor at the University of Northern Colorado, and often came to the festival back east to visit with his old friends and play music with them. They all went to college together at Bellarmine and enjoyed getting back together whenever they could.

"I haven't seen you guys in what, three years?" Doc said as he walked up and started hugging them. "What a sight for sore eyes."

"Dang, it's good to see you here," Ben said.

"Those things ain't doin' any good in the cases, Doc said. "Break 'em out. Let's show 'em how it's done."

"Can we use your bench, Woody?" Kevin asked.

"Yeah, yeah. Move that stuff out of the way."

Ben and Kevin laid their cases on Woody's workbench and got their guitars out.

"Let me look at that real quick," Woody said.

Ben handed him his Martin, and Woody looked closely at the neck, checking his work from the year before. "It seems to be holding pretty tight," Woody said. "Bring it by in the morning and I'll check the setup."

"Sure will," Ben said as he took the guitar and strapped it around his neck.

The music stopped. The bass player standing in the middle of the circle looked at them over in the corner.

"You guys got one?" he asked.

Doc looked at Ben and Kevin, and they all shook their heads in unison. "Yeah, we got one," Doc said. "Let's do *Wheel Hoss.*"

"Are you serious?" Ben asked. "It's been a while."

"Coward," Doc chuckled.

"Fine. Let's go."

They started playing the popular bluegrass instrumental at breakneck speed. Everyone around the fire went quiet as a few of the other musicians joined in, but struggled to keep up. It was an impressive display of musicianship as the three friends played together for the first time since Doc had moved to Colorado. As the last chord was played, the crowd let out a cheer that was heard all around the park. The festival was off to a great start.

Early the next morning, the door to the motorhome opened slowly as Darcy stepped out. She smiled when she noticed Ben lying on the cot once again, sound asleep. She turned to Trevor, who was still inside. "Yes, he's out here."

She shifted the cup of coffee into her other hand so she could close the door behind her as she eased her way down the two steps.

Darcy took her usual seat and sipped on her hot coffee while she looked around the campground, trying to determine who made it in while they slept. It was Friday morning, and she knew this is the day everyone normally shows up. Only the die-hards show up on Thursday and have to pay extra for the campsites.

There were a few people walking across the field from the tent camping area to the shower house. Others were busy lighting fires to get their coffee pots brewing and to start breakfast. It was always a peaceful time for Darcy. She just looked around, not saying a word, random thoughts coming and going. One was about her doctor's visit the week before. Then she remembered that she had her Bible under her arm. She smiled and opened it up with a reverence, like she was greeting God himself.

"Good morning," she said just under her breath as she turned to where she had left off reading the night before. She was reading from *John 17*, her favorite passage because it is Jesus actually praying, and because it is such a clear expression of the love He has for His entire united church.

"But now I come to You; and these things I speak in the world so that they may have My joy made full in themselves," she read. "John 17:13 has to be one of the most encouraging passages of hope," she thought. "*'My joy made full',*" she repeated. "How awesome it would be to experience His joy made full."

She took another sip of coffee as she peeked out over the opposite edge of her mug and saw the morning dew glistening just under a light layer of ground fog, the sun breaking over the horizon, causing the whole scene to glow.

A little white dog, some kind of terrier, was prancing through the tall grass, lifting its paws as high as they could go. Darcy sat the mug on the arm of the Adirondack chair and lowered her gaze back into her Bible. After she read for about twenty minutes, she heard footsteps in the grass coming around the back of the motorhome, and then a voice.

"Hey there, pretty girl!"

Darcy jolted her head up, and she put the palm of her hand over her mug so it wouldn't fall. "Oh my gosh, Doc! "She sprang from her chair, set the Bible and mug on the table, and lunged toward him, throwing her arms around his neck.

"How are you?" Doc smiled.

"Hey Trev," Darcy called out. "Come out here!"

Ben stirred on the cot, probably wondering what all the commotion was about.

"Dang, we've missed you," Darcy said as she held on to one of Doc's arms and walked him into the campsite.

"Ben! Get your butt up, son," Darcy said. "Look who's here."

"We actually jammed some last night over at Woody's place," Doc said.

"And I missed it?" Darcy said in a wistful tone, like a little girl who forgot to wake up for Christmas.

Ben rolled over and rubbed his eyes.

"Mornin," Doc said.

"Hey Doc. Kinda early, ain't it?"

"Maybe a little."

"Are you camped over there by Woody?" Darcy asked.

"Yeah, just came from there. He's already out setting up his workbench."

Trevor came outside with a dish towel draped over his shoulder and a bowl of fruit in his hand. "Hey man, how the heck are ya?"

"Doin' great, buddy," Doc said. "Good mornin'. Here, let me help you with that."

Doc took the bowl from Trevor and set it on the picnic table. By then, Ben was sitting up, rubbing his face. "Hey Trev, mind if I go grab a quick shower?" he asked.

"No, go for it."

Ben got up and walked slowly toward the door, patting Doc on the shoulder as he walked by. "That was some fun pickin' last night."

"Yes, it was," Doc said.

"I'm gonna go say hi to Woody," Darcy said. "I'll be back shortly to get breakfast going."

Trevor smiled and winked at her. "Tell him I'll see him later on."

Darcy headed out across the campground. She strolled slowly, taking in the sights and sounds and smells. She smiled and waved at those who were awake, starting fires and stoves, heating up the coffee and getting the frying pans sizzling hot for breakfast.

"Hey there, girl! I heard you a fiddlin' over there yesterday. Sounded real good. You wanna join us for breakfast?" someone said to Darcy.

"Oh no. I've got a bunch to feed back at the camp. Thank you, though."

Darcy kept walking slowly past the old beat up Airstream. She had seen it many times through the years. It had obviously seen a lot of bluegrass festivals.

She continued to walk down the lines of campers, waving at a few people even when she didn't know them. There were already a few old men sitting out on lawn chairs all alone next to a small camp fire, often playing a guitar or a banjo softly while sipping on their coffee. The festival was beginning to come awake for the day. Then she smelled bacon cooking, mixed with the perfume of the dew-laden wildflowers and dogwoods that lined the fence at the edge of the field. This quiet time was one of the things she loved about being at these festivals. Another thing she loved was the people. Oh how she loved her friends there.

As Darcy approached Woody's camp, she saw him out under the white tarp, setting up his instrument displays and the old workbench he used to repair and set-up thousands of fiddles at hundreds of bluegrass and old-time music festivals year after year. He was well known for being highly skilled, fair in his practices, and slow as molasses. Everyone loved Woody.

"Hey, bud," Darcy said as she approached the tent from behind him.

Woody lowered his arms from hanging a fiddle on his display wall and turned to see who was coming. "Well hey there, sweetie," he said with a wide tooth-filled grin on his face. "I am so happy to see you." He walked toward her with his arms raised.

"I'm happy to see you, too," she said with sparkling water-glazed eyes and a smile.

She walked into his open arms, and he gave her a long bear hug. Woody had known Darcy since she was a little girl learning to play the violin, and always kept tabs on her through her parents when she attended Bellarmine and the Conservatory. He couldn't have loved her more if she was his own daughter. He put his hands on her shoulders and pushed her away to arm's length, looking her over. "Baby girl, you get more beautiful every time I see you."

"Shut up," She giggled and stepped back into his bear hug.

When Woody started to loosen his embrace, Darcy held on tighter. Then he heard her crying. He had no idea what it was about, but he kept quiet and just let her cry.

After a while, she finally loosened her grip, and he motioned for her to have a seat. He pulled a lawn chair around in front of her and sat down. He tore a piece of a paper towel off a roll and handed it to her to wipe her face, then he leaned forward and wrapped both of his big hands around hers.

"What is it, hon?"

"I'm sorry," she said. "I didn't see that coming." Darcy then tear-fully explained the terrible news she received from her doctor the week before. Woody listened until she got the story, the anger, the frustration, and the tears out for him to repair. After she had finished telling her story, Woody allowed silence to highlight her pain.

After what seemed like a few minutes of simmering, Woody said, "Sweetie, I am so sorry. I know you wanted babies more than life itself. Is this a done deal? I mean, are they sure?"

"I guess they're as sure as they can be."

"Dang," Woody said. "I can't believe that."

"Well," Darcy said, and then paused to assess her words.

"What?" Woody asked.

"I'm almost afraid to say it." She paused and thought for a few seconds. "Do you think I've done something to make God mad? Why else would he do this?"

"Oh, honey, I wouldn't even think that. I know you're hurting, but I don't think God is punishing you. What would make you think such a thing?"

"I don't know. I just don't understand what's happening."

"Sweetie, you've been faithful to God all your life and you know he loves you. I think if you have a bone to pick, it'll be with Satan. We just can't know why God allows these things to happen. Have you discussed this with your pastor?"

"No. Not yet."

"You need to do that when you get back. You need the support of your church on this one," Woody said.

"I know. I will. I've just felt a little off about taking things to him lately. I don't know. I'm just not getting a good feeling about that church."

"Do you know Preacher Stan over there in that green motorhome?" Woody asked.

"No. Why?"

"You might want to have a chat with him. He's a good guy. I work on his banjo from time to time. Church of Christ preacher from West Virginia, but he's different than you would expect from most Church of Christ folks. He doesn't buy in to that whole idea that you're going to hell for playing instruments in church?"

"Churches really believe that?"

"Well yes, some do, among other things," he said. "You wanna go meet him? I see him sitting over there."

"I don't know." Darcy sighed.

"Come on. You'll like him." Woody stood up and walked toward the lane, then turned to see if Darcy was following him. She was.

"Mornin', preacher," Woody said as they walked up under the canopy of the pastor's motorhome.

"Well hey, hey, Woody! How the heck are you doin', man? Who we got here?" Stan said, as he stood up looking at Darcy.

Stan Radcliff was a Church of Christ preacher and a graduate of the Sunset School of Preaching in Lubbock, Texas. He and Woody had been friends for many years since Stan had been trying to teach himself to play the banjo.

"This is my sweet friend, Darcy Marshall. Fiddler extraordinaire," Woody said. "I've known her since she was a kid just learning how to play."

"Well, hello there, Darcy. Pleased to make your acquaintance."

"Good to meet you," Darcy said as she reached her hand out to shake his.

Preacher Stan, as everyone called him, and Woody chatted for a while, catching up on old times. Darcy listened patiently, learning some about the good ole days. Stan kept glancing over at her, apparently sensing that she had been crying. Woody must have brought her over to visit for a reason, but Stan didn't want to push it. "Listen to us being rude," he said to her.

"Oh, no. That's fine. I'm enjoying the stories," she said.

Stan looked in her eyes intently as if to read her mind. "So, young lady, what is your dream?"

Darcy looked over at Woody and then back to Preacher Stan. "What do you mean?" She smiled uneasily.

"Well, the way I see it, God plants the seed of a dream in all of us before we're even born. As a kid, God entrusts us with a gift to pursue that dream. Then as we mature, our dream grows into a full-on passion. If we use our gift the way God intends, that dream will become a reality. So what's your dream?"

Darcy turned away from the conversation and stared off into the woods nearby for a few short moments. "Well, let me think," she said. "I've always loved my fiddle. Even when I was learning to play classical violin, I could never wait to get home from school to get my hands on it. It's always been an extension of me, I guess."

"But you play bluegrass now?" he asked.

"Oh yes," she said. "I still play classical occasionally when some special event comes up. But yes, I love playing bluegrass. Lately, I've even grown to love old-time music. It just touches my heart and takes my breath away."

"Do you play fiddle contests?" Stan asked.

"Oh, I've played some band contests. I thought I might try the fiddle contest down at Athens again this year. Didn't do too good last year."

"Wow, that's a good one. That'll be fun. Have you heard of Weiser?"

Darcy was once again perplexed. "Have I heard of what?"

"Weiser, Idaho. It's probably the biggest fiddle contest in the country. You need to check it out."

"The biggest, huh? Oh! Come to think of it, I heard of that back in college. I thought that rung a bell. I never thought much about it. But it sounds pretty amazing. I'll look into it."

Then her smile faded and she looked to the ground. "But, I have some things I'm dealing with right now that I need to resolve before I can think about Athens or Weiser."

Stan frowned, his voice filled with concern when he asked, "Is there something I can help you with?"

She lifted her head and glanced at Woody. He smiled and nodded. Darcy then turned to Stan with a half-smile. "Well, maybe you can answer some questions for me."

She told him about what she had recently learned. She didn't notice that Woody had gotten up and walked back toward his tent. After Darcy explained her story, again, and through many tears, she was exhausted. But Preacher Stan was still listening intently, as if he cared, and maybe he really and truly did, even though they'd only just met. There was a kindness in his eyes, and that was nice. The pain of knowing she would never have her own children had been too much to bear, all too-consuming. Kindness was something she needed a lot of right now.

"I just don't understand why God would do this to me," Darcy said.

"Well, it's impossible to know why God does what he does when he does it," Stan said. "We just have to have faith that he knows what is best for us. You are a gifted young lady with a lot to offer. Maybe God wants you to focus on the gift for now. Or maybe he wants you to be someone else's mom. Have you considered adopting?"

Darcy froze.

"It may be too soon right now," Stan said. "But maybe someday, it'll be good for you and your husband to think about it."

She shook her head, her red puffy eyes staring back at his.

"Can I get you something to drink?" he asked.

Then Darcy noticed Woody was gone. She turned and saw him back across the lane.

"I guess he had things to do," Stan said.

"I guess so," she giggled. "No drink for me, thanks. I'm going to run by there and let him know I need to get back to camp. I've got mouths to feed. Thank you so much for listening to me babble on."

"Oh, think nothing of it. It was my pleasure. It's been really nice meeting you. Think about what I said and come back anytime. Sorry you missed my wife, Sue. Come by later on if you want. I'd like her to meet you. I'd like to hear you play, too."

"Sounds good, Stan. It's been a pleasure to meet you as well."

"One more thing before you go," he said. "Do you mind if I pray for you?"

Darcy was a little shocked, but she sat back down and took his hands. He prayed for her comfort. When he said "amen," she got up again with tears in her eyes and gave Preacher Stan a hug.

"Thank you so much," she said. "I do look forward to meeting your wife."

When Darcy passed by Woody's place, she said, "Thank you."

"Oh, no problem, sweetie. I thought you might like him."

"I really do," she said. "Woody, are you going to be at Athens this year?"

"I wouldn't miss it for the world. Haven't missed it for the last fifteen years."

"Good. I think I'm going to go and give it another try."

"You'll knock 'em dead," he said.

Darcy paused and turned. "Do you know those guys that are down here from Ohio? I think the band name is *Buckeye Bluegrass* or something like that."

"Yeah, I've seen 'em around. Why?"

"Do you know the guitar player?"

Woody curled up the corner of his mouth and gave her a deadpan look.

"Jack Hanford? Yeah, I know him. He's a good musician but he's pretty full of himself. He seems to be pretty convinced that he's God's gift to bluegrass. Have you had a run-in with him?"

"No. I was just thinking about the band contest at Athens and I know they're going to be competing. Ben seems to think we can take 'em."

"They're pretty good," Woody said. "But I think you'll be okay."

CHAPTER 3

Competing

"It is all about the bow, it is like a paintbrush."
~ David Game

The motorhome rolled lazily down Interstate 65, rocking back and forth as it caught gusts of wind, weaving around rusted-out pickup trucks, elderly drivers, and horse trailers. Trevor, wanting to give no indication that he might not be in full control, fought the thirty-five-foot beast to keep it in line. But he had white knuckles and a bead or two of sweat on his forehead.

A bright and sunny, but windy Thursday afternoon, traffic was light, for this part of Tennessee. A little wind with a vehicle the size of this felt like a tornado, especially at sixty miles an hour. Darcy had her choice of where to nest in the traveling hotel, either vertically or horizontally. But she chose to ride in the passenger seat next to Trevor. She tried to remain steady while she read a small paperback book, purposely ignoring the highway-dance going on around her.

Four months had passed since they learned that Darcy was unable to have children. They had talked about what Preacher Stan told her at the festival in Lexington and they were beginning to consider adoption.

"It says here that kids who are adopted normally don't consider it a big deal as long as it isn't just sprung on them later in life. It seems like they would feel like half of their story is missing," Darcy read.

She dropped back into silence, engrossed in her book, *So You Want to Adopt a Baby.* Trevor looked over at her and saw the concentration in her eyes. He smiled, looked to his left to check the rear view mirror, and then focused his eyes back on the road.

"Just about there," he said as he pulled the monster off of the interstate and onto the ramp near Judy's house. They had all decided that Judy would ride with them to Athens since they were going right through Nashville.

"Honey, how long do you think this will take?" Darcy asked as she continued to turn pages.

"Probably about twenty minutes if the traffic stays like it is."

Darcy's head popped up out of the book. First she looked straight ahead, and then she turned to give him a harsh stare, squinting her eyes, and chuckled. "Adoption, goober."

They both laughed as Trevor guided the motorhome onto the road leading to Judy's house. Darcy returned his smile and closed the booklet. She pitched it onto the dashboard and shifted her position forward in the seat, gathering clutter accumulated during the trip, placing it in a small bag.

"I love this time of year," she said. "I can't wait to see Judy. Should I tell her about all this adoption stuff?"

"I see no harm in it," Trevor said. "Frankly, I think you need to tell her. Have you decided whether or not to enter the fiddle contest this year? You know she's going to want you to."

"I don't know, Trev. It was so embarrassing last year."

"What embarrassing! You came in second place, for cryin' out loud!"

"I know, but I was kind of disappointed. Why don't we just do the band and leave it at that? I'd really like to beat those guys from Ohio."

Trevor chuckled. "If you're going to win the national fiddle championship, I'm pretty sure you'll have to enter some local contests. And besides, those people loved you last year. Forget what the judges had to say."

Darcy opened the storage compartment in the dashboard and pulled out the judge's comment sheet from the year before. She wanted to refresh her memory, as if she hadn't read it hundreds of times already.

"'You need to relax and smile more. Your delivery is excellent. Keep up the good work,'" she read aloud, mocking the judges with an exaggerated drawl. She put the paper down. "It was my first contest. What in the world did he expect?"

"Easy now." Trevor smiled. "Second place is nothing to sneeze at, especially for your first time." He paused and checked all of his rearview mirrors. "You're way too hard on yourself."

"I guess."

"You guess what? You guess you're way too hard on yourself or you guess you'll enter the contest?"

"I guess." She smiled and threw the piece of paper over her left shoulder into the floor behind her. She looked out the window at the fields where a young colt frolicked in a pond. It shook off the water and ran across the field like lightning. She leaned forward to continue watching as they passed by. When the horse was out of sight, she settled back into her seat and gazed into the distance, watching old farmhouses and horse stables pass by. The trees and grass were still a fresh green, even as fall was creeping in. "I love Tennessee," she whispered to herself.

As they pulled around the circle drive in front of the huge white antebellum house, Judy came running out of the front door to greet them. Her fiery red hair and big smile were a welcoming sight as they came to a stop. Darcy walked around her seat and opened the coach door to let Judy load in her belongings. Within just a few minutes, all three were on the road to Athens, Alabama. They hoped to be there in under two hours.

The trio arrived in Athens just as the sun was going down. It was Friday night and the crowds were beginning to arrive in anticipation of all the Saturday events. Trevor was directed to their camping space in the parking lot. There were all kinds of campers lined up, crammed together like sardines into a space never intended to be a campground. As they backed in, they could hear Kevin's blood curdling screams. He and Ben ran toward the motorhome.

"Oh, my Lord," Judy said.

"Good grief," Darcy quickly followed as they all laughed at the spectacle.

Darcy threw the door open just as Trevor brought the motorhome to a standstill. Ben and Kevin jumped aboard, yelling and laughing and greeting everyone with hugs. It was always a grand reunion with those two.

"We're on for the eliminations tonight," Ben said. "I think we're number three and we're right after Buckeye Bluegrass."

"Have you seen Jack yet?" Darcy asked, looking at both Ben and Kevin. Her face was twisted as if she had just taken a bite from a lemon.

"Well, yeah," Kevin said. "He was back there jamming a little while ago behind Founders Hall."

"I wonder if they'll mind a couple of girls joining in," Darcy said as she looked at Judy with a mischievous look. The girls laughed while Trevor, Ben, and Kevin all looked at each other, shaking their heads.

"Oh, this is going to be a crazy fun weekend," Ben said.

"Don't encourage them," Trevor warned.

"Hey, if you guys don't mind, I'm gonna run down to the registration desk while y'all set up camp," Darcy said.

"Uh...sure," Trevor said.

Darcy opened the door and jumped to the pavement. "I'll be back shortly."

"What's that all about?" Judy asked.

"Oh, I think I talked her into trying it again."

"YES!" the other three shouted in unison. "Yes!"

When Darcy left the registration table in the small utility building, she headed back up the hill to Founders Hall. She went toward the back of the building where she knew everyone would be congregating. There were a few jams going on while musicians waited to be called on stage for their two competition songs. Trevor and the others were under a tree where they had taken their instruments out of the cases, and were tuning. Darcy snuck up behind Trevor and poked him hard in the back. He jerked around, startled by her attack.

"You scared the crap out of me!"

"Sorry," she laughed.

"Well, did you do it?"

"I did it," she said. She looked at the ground and shook her head. "I did it."

"Stop." Trevor said. "You're going to be just fine. Your fiddle's over there if you want to get tuned up."

After everyone was tuned and had jammed for a while, they agreed it was time to make their way up to join the line of competitors that formed outside the back door of Founders Hall. The line was fairly long, and band members as well as old friends were talking and laughing, catching up on old times and sharing war stories of festivals and competitions past. Since they were going to be number three in the band competition, they weren't very far back in the line. All the members of Buckeye Bluegrass were just in front of them.

"Hey man! How are you doing?" Ben said, looking at Jack.

"Doing well. Good to see you guys here. Are you ready for this thing?" Jack glanced at the line, at Darcy standing behind Trevor, while Ben answered his question.

"Oh God," Darcy whispered to Trevor as she turned and looked the other way.

"Oh yeah, we're feeling pretty good about it," Ben said.

"I think we've got this nailed," Jack said.

"Probably so," Ben said. "Good luck to you guys." Ben turned around and grinned at Trevor and Darcy standing behind him, trying not to laugh.

The first band was on stage, and everyone in line could hear the applause echoing around the building from the hundreds of bluegrass and old-time music fans sitting in rows of lawn chairs in the front yard. One of the volunteers walked out of the back door and motioned for Jack and his band to come inside the building.

"I hope they nail it!" Judy said.

"Shhhhhhhh," Darcy said as all five of them busted out laughing, fearing, yet almost hoping, that Jack might hear them.

"What a piece of work," Kevin said, shaking his head and leaning against his tall standup bass fiddle.

Again, a loud applause echoed throughout the campus as the first band left the stage, which was actually the huge front porch of Founders Hall, lined by tall Grecian white columns.

A few minutes later, the volunteer again motioned to Trevor to have the band come into the building and prepare to go on stage. They walked up the concrete steps through a set of old creaky double doors and down a short hallway. The ancient boards in the hardwood floors were wide and loose, and squeaked loudly every time someone walked on them. It was a little embarrassing. They hoped the noise wasn't loud enough to be heard on stage. The front door that led to the porch was straight ahead and only a short walk through the heart of the old building, just through the large reception room where an antique grand piano sat among several paintings on the wall of people presumably associated with the college down through history. The furniture was plush, and blended with the architecture of the building.

As they waited, they could clearly hear the proceedings on stage. They could even see the backs of a couple of band members playing, and out into the yard where the music fans sat. The music stopped.

"All the way from Cincinnati, Ohio, Buckeye Bluegrass!" the emcee shouted.

The crowd cheered, and some even stood, apparently trying to start an ovation. It was a bit odd for a competition and highly discouraged. The Buckeye Bluegrass band walked back through the double doors in the front of the building, past Trevor and the rest of the band.

"Next up, ladies and gentlemen, is Fiddler's Roost," the emcee said into the microphone.

The volunteer motioned for the band to head out onto the front porch to take their positions. They filed out and went to their microphones. Everyone took in a deep breath as Trevor nodded his head toward the emcee.

"Ladies and gentlemen, let's hear it for Fiddler's Roost doin' *Sally Goodin!*"

Darcy quickly tucked her fiddle under her chin and raised the bow for a quick shuffle kickoff on this old instrumental tune. They played the tune faster than most bands, with a flawless execution of their own arrangement. After Darcy played the tune, Trevor took over on a banjo break, followed by Judy on the mandolin and Ben on his guitar. After they had all played their parts, the lead returned to Darcy. She played at lightning speed with impeccable accuracy. When she peeked at the audience briefly, she saw faces turned to her in rapt attention, some swaying gently to the music.

She smiled. Her long blonde hair sparkled as she jerked her head left and right, swinging her hips and tapping her foot in time with the cadence of Kevin's standup bass. As she drew her bow across the final note and the others came to an abrupt stop in perfect time, the crowd erupted into applause and shouts of approval. Darcy grinned at Trevor, her beautiful smile stretching from ear to ear.

"You ready?" Trevor mouthed.

She couldn't hear him but easily knew what he'd said. She looked down the line of her bandmates and raised her eyebrows, getting confirmation from everyone that they too were ready for the next song. She nodded again, looking at Trevor.

"This next tune is called *Cryin' Holy,*" Trevor said as he started his banjo roll to lead the group into the song. "Cryin' holy unto the Lord. Cryin' holy unto the Lord. For if I could I surely would stand on that rock...where Moses stood."

Smiles came over the faces of the crowd and feet began to tap to the quick rhythm of the beat. Darcy took the first instrumental break on the fiddle according to plan. The band knew this would be in front of an audience of fiddle lovers, so as they built their set list, they agreed this would be the best sequence for the arrangement. She executed her break flawlessly to a rousing applause. The song continued into the next verse and chorus, followed another perfectly executed break by Judy on the mandolin, then the final chorus and banjo break by Trevor.

When the last note rang out, the audience jumped to their feet with a loud ovation, whistling and clapping their hands over their heads. It was a thunderous roar. Trevor, Darcy, Ben, Judy, and Kevin lined up close together and took a deep bow, then walked off the porch in single file, looping around behind one of the tall white columns and back into the door they came out of.

"That was great!" someone said.

It came from a girl who was with the next band waiting to go on stage. The group continued on through the foyer and out the back door. Smiles were beaming as they walked down the steps and onto the sidewalk that led down the hill to the parking lot.

"Well, that was fun," Judy said.

"I thought it was awesome!" Kevin shouted.

"I don't even know when they announce the finalists for tomorrow," Ben said. "When do we need to come back up here?"

Trevor pulled the schedule from his back pocket and looked it over. "I guess we need to be back at nine o'clock, right after the junior fiddlers." He paused and looked at Darcy. "I think we'll be up there anyway." He smiled at her.

"Yes, yes. I'm in. I registered a little while ago," Darcy said.

"REALLY!" Judy shrieked. She wrapped an arm around Darcy's shoulders as they continued to clumsily walk down the hillside. "Yes!"

They all ate supper and tried to relax as their heart rates settled back into a normal rhythm. Darcy could think of only one thing now. She sat with the fiddle in her arms, not playing it, not tuning it, just sitting with her cheek against the neck and the body of it resting in her lap. In a daze, her contorted face pressed up into her eye.

"You're doing O.B.S., right?" Ben said.

"Oh, crap, I don't even know!" Darcy said.

Trevor laughed. "You have to do your version of it so they know what you can do. You only get one tune, ya know."

"I know, I know."

"You play O.B.S. and I'll borrow Ben's guitar and go up there with you," Trevor said.

An hour later, Darcy found herself on stage again with bright lights shining on her. It was cool and a little damp, so she couldn't help but worry about her strings. She could barely see the crowd in front of her through the glare. Judy, Ben, and Kevin stood in the back of the crowd, watching Darcy's every move.

The emcee stood on the front edge of the stage. "Ladies and gentlemen, little Miss Darcy Marshall playing the old *Orange Blossom Special!*"

The crowd cheered, and Darcy glanced over at Trevor who was holding his guitar at the ready.

"Kick it off, hon," he said.

She smiled at him. "Love you," she said, just moving her lips, and nodded.

He smiled back at her. "Knock 'em dead, babe," he said.

Darcy turned to the crowd, stepped up to the microphone, and raised the fiddle to her chin, bow to the strings. She took a deep breath, paused, and then shoved the bow down.

At first, she played with a quick back-and-forth shuffle to set the tempo and get the feel for the tune. Then, she began to emulate a train-whistle's long sinking notes, flowing steady and rock solid. Darcy could feel the music in her soul. Her foot started tapping and her hips bounced in time with Trevor's rhythm. A small cloud of rosin dust reflecting the light formed around her fiddle. When she sensed the tension and anticipation of the crowd, the tune well on its way, she ripped through the notes of the melody like nothing she'd ever done before. She glanced at her friends standing in back with their mouths gaping open.

Her performance was flawless, and she knew it. The music took her breath away. Darcy executed her rendition of *The Orange Blossom Special* with amazing speed, grace, agility, and clarity.

Trevor kept playing hard and steady on the bass notes and down strokes on Ben's guitar. A banjo player at heart, Trevor was quite an accomplished rhythm guitar player as well, and proved it that night. This couple on stage, just the two of them, playing under the bright lights, was magical. Three rounds of the melody, a quick A-run on the guitar, followed by a long low A note on the fiddle, and it was over. The crowd roared to their feet. All the clapping, cheering, shouting, and whistling, was overwhelming.

Trevor stepped back a couple of steps, without Darcy noticing, and pointed at her. The crowd cheered louder. Darcy turned to look at Trevor only to find that he wasn't there. She dropped her jaw and began looking around frantically. She finally saw him standing almost behind her. She smiled in relief and reached for his hand to pull him to the front of the stage with her. She was in tears, and they kissed. The crowd loved it. Darcy's new fans roared again. The Marshalls were now, officially, the sweethearts of the contest.

After what seemed an eternity, Trevor and Darcy took their final bow, headed through the door into the hallway, and pranced down the back steps. They heard the emcee take the microphone.

"Unbelievable. Simply unbelievable!" he shouted.

Cheers and whistles continued. Judy ran up to Darcy out of breath, partially because of her yelling and partially from running around the audience and Founders Hall to get to her.

"Jesus Christ, you were on fire!" Judy screamed as she wrapped her arms around Darcy's neck. "That was amazing, sweetie."

Ben and Kevin were close behind, whooping and laughing, pointing their fingers at her. "We know that woman!" Ben shouted. "I'm sure she's forgotten who we are, but we know that woman!"

"Kiss my butt," Darcy said, laughing, still in a state of shock.

"No, really Darcy," Judy said. "You looked like an angel in a cowboy hat."

"Yes, you did," Kevin said.

They all walked back to the camp together as their ears rang in the quiet of the evening. Basking in the afterglow, Judy plugged in the coffee maker and took some snacks out as the others sat around a folding table, laughing and comparing notes. Judy was passing around coffee cups when she looked up. Darcy followed Judy's gaze and saw Jack Hanford and his band walking by. He glanced at them with an awkward grin on his face.

"Nice job," Jack said. "We'll see you for the finals tomorrow."

He turned toward his companions and whispered something Darcy couldn't hear, and they giggled like schoolboys before walking away. Darcy shook her head, threw her hat on the table, and reached for her coffee cup.

The next evening, the awards were announced. No surprise to anyone, Darcy Marshall took home the first place trophy for Junior Fiddle. When she walked onto the stage to collect it, along with her five-hundred-dollar check, she had tears in her eyes. "I want to thank my husband, Trevor, and my band, Fiddler's Roost, for getting me through that," she said.

The emcee and the crowd chuckled and applauded.

"That little girl is going places," the emcee said as Darcy walked off of the stage.

When the band competition results were announced, Fiddler's Roost came in second place. Ben went on stage to get the trophy since Darcy said she was too embarrassed to go up again. But everyone had happily accepted the fact that this was her band.

The first place band, Buckeye Bluegrass, was clearly a talented group of musicians. But Darcy still had a sour taste in her mouth from Jack's arrogance and his badmouthing her the year before.

"I'm really sorry we didn't win," Darcy said as they walked back to the camp.

"What in the world are you talkin' about, girl?" Kevin shouted. "You're the fiddle queen, for cryin' out loud! I'd say we won big time!"

"You got that right," Ben said.

"Second place is just fine for the band," Trevor said. "Watching you kick butt on that stage last night made it worth everything we've put into this. Just think of how you feel right now and multiply that by ten for the nationals in Weiser."

She smiled and wrapped an arm around Trevor's waist and laid her head on the side of his chest as they continued to walk.

"I can't even imagine what that must be like," she said in her soft, dreamy voice.

"We'll get 'em next year," Judy said.

Darcy's mind drifted from the conversation. "Next year," she repeated softly to herself. She wasn't even thinking about her music.

CHAPTER 4

Receiving

"Music is the art of the prophets and the gift of God."
~ Martin Luther

On Sunday morning, Trevor, Darcy, and Judy said their good-byes to Ben and Kevin, packed up the motorhome and drove out to I-65 headed north, back to Nashville. It was a sleepy trip back home and few words were spoken.

Darcy and Trevor rested for a few minutes at Judy's house after they unloaded her belongings and spoke about the weekend. They all agreed it had been a fun time.

When they arrived home, Trevor backed the motorhome along the side of the old white, well-maintained bungalow with a massive front porch. He backed it into the space on the side of the small garage in the back yard.

"Let's take a nap first, then we can come unload everything," Darcy said as she picked up her fiddle case from behind her seat and climbed down out of the cockpit. "I'm exhausted."

Trevor walked back into the coach, picked up his banjo, and went out through the back door. Just as they were reaching the house, Darcy heard ringing. "Oh crap, it's the phone," she said.

Trevor scrambled to retrieve the key from under the door mat. He barely had the door open when Darcy rushed in under his arm to answer the call.

"Hello?" she said.

"Oh, hi! How are you guys doing?"

"Yes, we just walked in the door."

Darcy turned to Trevor and mouthed, "It's Annette."

"From church?" he whispered.

She shook her head and stood, frozen, listening to the caller while staring at the wall.

Trevor continued walking through the kitchen toward the music room with his banjo, nabbing Darcy's fiddle from her as he walked by.

"Really?" Darcy asked. "Are you sure?"

"How old is the mother? Is she good with it?"

"Oh, she does?"

"Oh my."

Trevor came back into the kitchen and sat at the table with a small stack of mail. Darcy tried to stifle the sob rising in her throat, her eyes filling with tears, but to no avail. Trevor noticed. He stared at her as she held her hand up, indicating for him to wait.

"Can I talk to Trevor and call you back?"

"Okay, great. I'll call you in a few minutes. Thank you."

"Uh huh. Bye."

Darcy covered her mouth with one hand and hung up the phone with the other. She walked quickly over to the table with a muffled squeal, and sat down across from Trevor. "Oh my God, Trevor!"

"Well, what, honey?"

"That was Annette, from church..." She paused and looked around at nothing, obviously in deep thought, or panic.

"Yes, you already told me that," he said.

"She said some relatives of theirs told them at church this morning that their single daughter is pregnant with her second child and they can't keep it. They're looking for someone to adopt the baby!"

Trevor's face lit up with a big smile, and his eyes filled with tears. "Is that right?" he said quietly.

"What do you think?" Darcy asked.

"Well, honey, I think we have to go talk to 'em!"

"Oh God, yes!" she said as they both stood and wrapped their arms around each other.

"I can't believe this," Darcy said, her cry muffled against Trevor's chest. She pulled her head away and looked into his eyes. "Are you sure, Trevor? Are you sure?"

"Honey, this is what you've been praying for. Call her back and find out when we can meet these folks."

On Wednesday evening, as Trevor and Darcy were driving to church, there was complete silence in the car. Trevor didn't normally go with her to church, but this was different. They were going to finally meet the parents of this young mother who had decided to give away her baby. Darcy broke the silence.

"I can't imagine what it must feel like to have to give away your child," Darcy said.

"Well, we don't really know the circumstances."

"No, we don't. But still. That poor girl. She must be devastated."

"Yeah. Probably so."

After they arrived at the church near where they lived, but a little closer to downtown Prestonsburg, Kentucky, they immediately found Annette and her husband Rudy. After the hugs and handshakes, Annette led them to the other side of the auditorium to introduce them to the parents of the young mother.

"Bob and Gladys Bartlett, this is Trevor and Darcy Marshall, the couple I told you about."

"It's so nice to finally meet you," Gladys said.

Darcy noticed that she seemed nervous, almost sad. Understandable, she thought, as they all shook hands.

"If you like, we can all go to our house after church, Gladys said, so you can meet our daughter, Mary Alice."

"That would be really nice," Darcy said.

They all sat together in a pew near the front. The preacher, Dave Jenson, was about to start his lesson when he looked over and saw the group sitting together. He smiled. He clearly knew what was going on. But then Darcy noticed the preacher's gaze settled on Trevor, and the smile on his face faded. Darcy knew the preacher hadn't seen Trevor in a long time. Maybe never in church.

Preacher Dave started his lesson, so Darcy sat up straighter to pay attention. It was about the importance of being a Christian, about salvation, and fellowship. They were all of the things that Darcy knew Trevor needed to hear. It was as if the man was trying to speak right at Trevor. Meanwhile, Trevor kept looking at Darcy, and shaking his head. Darcy could only smile and squeeze his hand.

After church, everyone told Preacher Dave what a good message it was, and then they retreated to the parking lot to head to the Bartlett's home, out on the edge of town.

Bob opened the front door to their house and everyone followed him in. "Mary Alice! We're home, honey. We have visitors," he said.

"Please have a seat and make yourselves at home," Bob said, motioning to the others.

Darcy felt her stomach churn. She was nervous, and for good reason.

Gladys piped up. "I'll get the brownies I made this afternoon. Coffee, anyone?"

"That would be great," Trevor said.

"Yes, please," Annette said, gesturing to Rudy and herself.

"None for me, thanks," Darcy said as she sat on a small love seat next to what looked like a potted tree in the corner of the living room.

Mary Alice walked into the room with a forced smile. Darcy noticed her eyes were puffy as though she had been crying. Darcy and Mary Alice immediately caught each other's gaze.

"Hi, honey," Gladys said. "These are the Marshalls. This is Trevor, and that's Darcy over there."

"Hello," Mary Alice said in a soft voice. Everyone greeted her much too gently.

She sat on the love seat next to Darcy, who intuitively took Mary Alice's hand in her own and held it there on her knee. "How are you doing?" Darcy said, looking deep into Mary Alice's eyes.

"I'm fine."

Just as an awkward silence fell over the room, tiny footsteps clambering down the hallway interrupted them.

"There she is!" Gladys beamed. "This here is little Miss Wendy."

Everyone smiled and laughed, talking to the baby girl. She was barely walking but circled the room to greet everyone. Annette reached out her arms, offering to pick her up, but Wendy quickly turned and ran away. "Oh, no. She doesn't want any part of that," Annette laughed.

Wendy walked over to Mary Alice and leaned on her knees. Her mother rubbed her back and smiled. "This is my joy," Mary Alice said. Her eyes welled up in tears, but she seemed to be holding them back.

Darcy looked at Gladys, waiting to get her attention. When Gladys met her eyes, she asked, "Would it be okay if I chatted with Mary Alice alone?"

"Of course," Gladys said.

Darcy turned to Mary Alice. "Is that okay?"

"Yeah, that's fine."

"Okay everyone, let's retire to the dining room," Gladys said. "The coffee and brownies are ready. Come on in here with me, Wendy, honey. Let's get a brownie."

The toddler wiggled across the living room floor toward Gladys, and the rest followed the two of them out of the room. Darcy was still holding Mary Alice's hand. The room got quiet quickly as the group moved to the back of the house.

"So, you can't have kids?" Mary Alice asked, nervously breaking the silence.

Darcy smiled. "No. The good Lord didn't see fit to have a baby maker in me."

"That must be hard."

"It is. But I take what God hands me. So are you really okay?"

Mary Alice dropped her head, obviously still holding back tears. "I know I have to give this baby up. But that too, is hard."

"I understand, sweetie," Darcy said, squeezing Mary Alice's hand tighter. "Are you sure this is what you want to do?"

"Oh yes. I've talked to mom and daddy about it a lot. They've been great with Wendy and all. They've been my saviors, actually. But this is asking too much. I didn't mean for this to happen."

"It's okay, sweetie. I know. We all make mistakes. God has a plan for all of us, and apparently, that plan includes another baby."

"I cry all the time. I know I'm driving them crazy."

"Don't worry about that, Mary Alice. They love you and they don't like seeing their little girl hurting. But this is a big deal, and overwhelming, I'm sure."

"I know they do." Mary Alice lowered her head again and wept.

"Look, sweetie," Darcy said. "I've always had this dream of being a big deal national champion fiddler. But I promised God I would give that all up for the chance to be a mother. Since I can't have children, I can only imagine that God wants me to raise someone else's child. If we adopt your baby, I promise the child will always know they have another family—that they were adopted. This child will always be part of your family, too."

"Really?" Mary Alice said, raising her head and squinting into Darcy's eyes. "I hadn't even thought of that. I just assumed my baby would be gone from me forever."

"No, honey. As strongly as I feel about motherhood, I can't imagine what it would be like to just give my baby away, thinking I would never see it again."

Mary Alice began to tear up again and leaned into Darcy, putting her arms around her in a tight embrace.

"I am so glad you came," Mary Alice whispered with a whimper.

"Me too, sweetie. Me too."

Trevor and Darcy arrived home around ten that night. The couple didn't speak a word all the way home. As soon as they walked into the living room, they sat and deeply exhaled in unison.

"Whew! Now what?" Trevor said. "We're going to have a baby." He smiled, almost giddy, and looked over at Darcy. "You okay?" he asked.

"Honey, I'm tired, I'm excited, and I'm terrified," Darcy said while staring off into the ceiling.

"What do you mean?"

"That little girl is scared to death," Darcy said. "I feel so badly for her. On one hand, I'm excited about adopting this baby. On the other hand, I could scream. Mary Alice could still change her mind."

Trevor slid down the length of the couch and put his arm around Darcy. "Yes, she could. But with little Wendy and her parents, she knows it's the right thing to do. You telling her that the baby will always know her—I think that was a great comfort to her."

"I just don't want the baby growing up under a cloud of lies, and thinking about how Mary Alice feels breaks my heart. She seems like such a gentle, loving soul."

"Yes, yes she does," Trevor said. "You okay then? I'm going to go jump in the shower."

"Yes, I'm fine. You go ahead."

After Trevor finished with his shower and dried off, he walked out of the bathroom and heard Darcy playing the sweetest melody on her fiddle. He stopped and listened. His heart melted at what seemed to be some sort of lullaby she was playing back in the music room.

"Wow," he whispered to himself. He froze with a tear streaking down his cheek. Then he wrapped himself in his robe and walked into the music room just as Darcy pulled her bow across the last note.

"That was really nice," Trevor said. "What was that?"

"I don't know. Just some tune that came to me." Darcy looked up at Trevor and smiled. Her face, soft and dimly lit from the side, put a smile on Trevor's face as well. "We're really going to do this, aren't we?" she asked.

"Yes, honey. We really are."

Seven months later, in January, Tracy Annette Marshall was born to Mary Alice, with her grandparents and her new parents, Trevor and Darcy, sitting nearby in the waiting room.

"Come see your new baby girl," the nurse said as she invited everyone back to the recovery room.

When they walked in, Darcy began to cry, overwhelmed with joy. She looked at the baby and smiled, then leaned over and kissed Mary Alice on the forehead. "She's so beautiful," Darcy said. "My God, she looks like the Bartlett family, for sure. Look at that black hair!"

The room was filled with joy and laughter and tears, except for Mary Alice. Darcy knew that she was about to do the hardest thing she had ever done. Her tears were coming from a deeper place.

"When can I go home to Wendy?" Mary Alice asked.

"It'll be a couple days, honey," Gladys said.

"We'll be right outside, sweetie," Darcy said.

She took Trevor by the arm, and they walked out of the room and down to the end of the hall where a large window overlooked the town. She thought Mary Alice might want to be alone with her parents.

"This is going to be so hard for her," Darcy said as she sobbed. "Yeah, I know it is. But she'll be fine. She's a strong young lady."

They took the baby home after a long, painful goodbye with the Bartlett family at the front door of the hospital. But then, it was time to be happy and enjoy their new little blessing.

When they got home, Trevor opened the back door and Darcy carried baby Tracy into the newly decorated nursery right next to their bedroom. Life was so good, but they couldn't have known that it was about to get even better. Two months later, Darcy was pregnant.

"What!" Darcy said to the doctor. "But wait...what?" She was speechless.

"We double-checked everything," the doctor said. "You, my dear, are going to have a baby."

"Are you sure? But...how can that be?"

"I don't know for certain, but we have seen many women get pregnant when they relax and stop trying so hard. Maybe when you and Trevor took Tracy home, it changed your outlook, and your body chemistry."

"Oh, my God!" Darcy shouted as she and the doctor both stood. Darcy threw her arms around his neck. "I can't believe this!"

"Well, believe it, my dear. You need to get home and tell Trevor the good news."

When Darcy got home, she walked through the back door and into the kitchen. She hung her keys and jacket on the hooks behind the door. "Trevor?"

"In here, honey," he said.

She found him in the living room. He was rocking the baby while watching a music video on TV. She stared at him with a smile, and was clearly about to pop when she took a seat on the couch, looking across the room at him.

"There is no way you're going to believe this," she began.

"Well, what?"

"I...I...I, oh my God."

"What, Darcy?" Trevor started to laugh.

"I'm pregnant!"

"What?"

"It's true. We're going to have a baby."

"Wait. How can that be?"

"I really don't understand it either, Trevor. But right now, I don't even care about how."

They both stood and embraced, laughing together and crying together, trying not to crush baby Tracy. "That's great," Trevor cried. "I can't believe this."

In December of that year, Darcy had another baby girl, Dawn Marshall. Tracy had a little sister. Not only were they sisters, they grew up being best friends. It was almost funny to see them frolicking together, one blonde, the other as dark-headed as could be.

As Tracy grew into a beautiful young lady, her mom's fiddle was everything to her. As soon as her hands were big enough to hold a bow, Darcy began teaching her everything she could. The four of them continued to go to the bluegrass festival every year across the state in Lexington, and Darcy continued to win contests at Athens, never forgetting about her dream to win at Weiser. When Tracy really caught the music bug, she was ten.

"Mommy, can I enter the fiddle competition at Athens this year?"

Darcy was stunned, but not really surprised. She just didn't know if it would ever come up. Deep down, she was elated. "I think that's a great idea, honey. But you better go ask your daddy."

Tracy took off toward the music room, and Darcy couldn't help but smile with a little tear in her eye. That little black-haired baby, with the captivating eyes and those gorgeous dimples was truly the gift from God that she had prayed for all those years. She cupped her hands together and dropped her head. "Thank you, God, for my little treasures."

Darcy eventually followed Tracy into the music room where Trevor had been working on some recordings. Tracy was sitting on his lap, her arm around his neck. They were both smiling from ear to ear. Dawn was sitting in a chair in the corner, drawing in her coloring book.

"You think she's ready?" Trevor asked.

They both looked at Darcy, Tracy shaking her head up and down, clearly trying to influence the conversation.

"Oh, I think she's more than ready."

"Heck yes, she's ready!" Dawn shouted.

Tracy threw her arms straight up in a goal-post victory stance, and then hugged her dad. Tracy and Dawn both got down from their chairs and embraced, jumping up and down.

"Yes, yes, yes!" they sang together.

In June, the family packed up the motorhome and headed to the bluegrass festival at the Kentucky Horse Park as they did every year. As soon as they hit the road, out came Tracy's fiddle. She loved to play for the family and sing with her mom and dad all the way across the state. Dawn would take out a book to read or a coloring book while biding her time, humming along and tapping her foot to the beat. She loved the music her family made but was never really interested in playing an instrument. Every now and then she would put her books aside and go up front to sing with them. She too had a beautiful voice.

As they set up camp, the girls helped their mom with things on the inside while Trevor tended to the chores outside, hooking up water and electric, raising the canopy, cleaning the picnic table, and such. The weather was perfect this time. It was known to rain at this festival on occasion, but not this year.

"Hey, good lookin'," Judy said as she came into the camp.

"Hey girl," Trevor said. He stopped what he was doing and gave her a hug.

"Where are all those beautiful women?" she asked.

"Aunt Judy!" Dawn squealed as she and Tracy jumped out of the motorhome.

"There's my girls." They wrapped themselves around her waist. Darcy came outside with a dish of food in each hand.

"Hey, sweetie." Judy nodded at Darcy. "Need some help?"

"No. Just a hug," Darcy said as she set the dishes on the picnic table and turned to put her arms around Judy's neck. "Sure have missed you."

"You too, darlin'."

"There's my favorite fiddle player," Ben said as he joined the group.

Tracy beamed. "Uncle Ben!"

Ben squatted down a little, and both of the girls ran into his arms. "Y'all ready to play some?" Ben asked.

Everyone else just waved and smiled.

"I'll go get Tracy's fiddle," Dawn said. She ran back into the motorhome, full of excitement. She loved to hear her sister play that fiddle, especially with her Uncle Ben.

"Where's that knot-head bass player?" Trevor asked.

"He called me yesterday," Judy said. "Said he'd be in a little late. Something about work."

Ben took his guitar out of its case and started tuning.

"Hey man, I brought that old clawhammer banjo of mine if you want to mess with it," Trevor said.

"Really? Heck yes," Ben said. "I love that old thing."

"I'll get it," Darcy said. "I'm going back in anyway."

Dawn came jumping out of the motorhome with Tracy's fiddle, and Darcy grabbed the door to keep it from banging against its side.

"Slow down, sweetie," Darcy said. "You don't want to hurt yourself...or that fiddle."

Darcy turned and shook her head, grinning at Trevor and Judy as she pulled the screen door closed behind her.

Trevor and Darcy had bought an old, way too expensive, fiddle from Woody on Tracy's ninth birthday. It was a beautiful instrument, way beyond what a typical child would own. But Darcy knew it was in Tracy's blood and wanted to give her every advantage.

Ben put his guitar away and stood to get the old, beat-up banjo case from Darcy. Tracy took her fiddle out of the case. She tightened the bow and rosined it up, then started tuning.

"You got any old-time tunes you've been working on, Trace?" Ben asked.

"Hey Tracy, do that tune you've been working up for the contest," Darcy said through the screen door.

"Contest?" Ben asked.

"Yes, I'm going to play at Athens this year," Tracy said.

"Holy mackerel," Ben said. "That is so cool." He shot his hand up and they met for a high-five.

"What's the tune?" Ben asked as he plucked on the old openback banjo.

"*Bonaparte's Retreat.* Do you know it?" Tracy asked.

"I love that tune," Ben said. "I think I can do something with you on this thing."

Ben sat on the edge of the picnic table, and Tracy walked over with her fiddle and stood facing him.

"Oh, wait. I have to tune this thing down for that," she said.

Ben frailed around, using the old-time clawhammer style strumming pattern, to get warmed up while Tracy re-tuned her fiddle.

"That's an old Celtic tune. What is that you're going to? Open D?"

"Yep. It's in D."

"Okay, perfect," Ben said.

Trevor finished up his setup duties and Darcy handed more food out the door to Judy. Ben and Tracy finally got tuned up and settled in.

"Okay, baby girl. Kick it off," Ben said.

Tracy glided her bow over the strings a few times as Dawn sat on top of the picnic table, next to Ben. Tracy dug in on her fiddle and lit the whole place up. Dawn started rocking her knees back and forth, tapping her foot on the seat of the picnic table. After Tracy played the first several phrases of the tune, Ben joined in, frailing the old banjo. It wasn't your typical jam music for a blue-grass festival, so their playing immediately drew the attention of the crowds walking by. Many folks gathered around the camp to listen to this little prodigy on her fiddle.

Darcy stepped down from the motorhome, beaming with pride, and motioned for people to come help themselves to the snacks she had just laid out.

"My God, Darcy. She's becoming someone else, isn't she?" Judy said softly.

"Oh yes. She's learning so fast. It just seems like yesterday that she couldn't reach far enough to get the bow across the strings."

Tracy's foot was tapping and her little hips were swaying to the tempo of the tune. Her eyes glanced back and forth between her strings and Ben, often watching what his fretting hand was doing on the banjo. Trevor walked up behind Darcy and Judy and put an arm around each of them.

"Our little girl is smokin' today," he said.

"It's amazing," Judy said. "You'd never know she was adopted. That only comes from blood."

"Well, some of the Bartletts are big in music as well, I'm told," Darcy said. "So, it isn't surprising. We are so blessed."

Trevor looked at Darcy. "Lucky, maybe," he said, and walked over to the picnic table.

Tracy ended the tune with a long pull on the D. She and Ben smiled at each other as the crowd that had been standing around, erupted into applause. Judy walked over and hugged Tracy.

"That was amazing!"

"Thank you, Aunt Judy. That's one of the tunes I'll be doing at Athens."

"Your mom told me you were going to do it. That's so exciting. You're going to do great."

"Well, if God is willing," Tracy said with a radiant dimpled smile.

Darcy looked at Judy, beaming again—so proud of her godly little girl.

When the crowd saw Ben and Tracy putting their instruments back in their cases, they slowly scattered in different directions. Darcy caught a glimpse of Jack Hanford looking at her, shaking his head. He paused for a few seconds before walking away with the rest.

CHAPTER 5

Performing

"If a feller can't bow, he'll never make a fiddler.
He might make a violin player, but he'll never make no fiddler."
~ Tommy Jarrell, Fiddler

In the coolness of the evening, Darcy and Trevor could hear cacophony of banjos and fiddles echoing back and forth in the park. It was a sound they had heard so many times before and learned to cherish. This was their silence, their calm. The girls had gone to bed and the campsite was dark. They were sitting on a bench just outside the door, leaning against the side of the motorhome.

"Honey, I've been thinking about something," Darcy said.

"What's that?"

"Well, I've been thinking Tracy is ready to play with the band."

"The band?"

"Our band. She loves playing with Ben, and Lord knows she can carry her own. What do you think about letting her do the show tomorrow?"

There was silence again, except for the music wafting softly through the trees, as Trevor thought the proposition over. Darcy finally looked over at him and took his hand, holding it on her knee.

"Are you sure about this?" Trevor finally said. "What about your dream? What about Weiser?"

"All that can wait. She's having such a good time, and I absolutely love watching her light up when she's playing with those guys. Judy can make sure she's okay on stage."

"Why don't you just both play?"

"Oh, I don't think so. I just want to see her fly. You guys can be the wind beneath her wings."

"I know. But I hate to see you stop. People love your playing too, ya know. Even me, on occasion."

"Shut up." Darcy giggled. It's not like I'm going to stop playing. And I'll still be teaching her."

"Hey guys," Kevin said, quietly walking in from the dark.

"Hey man, you finally made it," Trevor said, reaching his hand out to shake Kevin's.

Darcy stood and wrapped her arms around Kevin's neck. "I'm so glad you're here."

"Me too," Kevin said.

"Have a seat," Trevor said. "Darcy was just talking to me about Tracy replacing her in the band."

"What?" Kevin said loudly, almost laughing as he sat down.

"Shhhhh," Darcy snapped. "The girls are sleeping."

"Is she doing that well?" Kevin asked.

"She's pretty amazing," Trevor said.

"She knows all my material," Darcy said.

After several more minutes of silence, Kevin said, "Wow. If that's what you guys want to do, I guess it's okay with me. Let's try it out."

They all leaned back and let the silence fill the campsite once again. Darcy laid her head back and gazed up at the stars through the black of the tree limbs.

"Ladies and gentlemen, Fiddler's Roost!" the emcee announced as Trevor, Ben, Judy, Kevin, and little Tracy walked onto the stage.

Everyone had agreed that morning that Tracy would play the show while the band considered how things go. Tracy just about jumped out of her skin with excitement when her mom told her. Once again, she and Dawn embraced and jumped up and down together as they had so many times before when one was celebrating for the other.

"Thank you," Trevor said as the applause quieted. "You all may notice something a little different up here this year. And I put the emphasis on LITTLE." A subtle wave of laughter broke the silence. Trevor continued. "Our usual fiddler, Darcy, has decided to take a break today and asked our oldest daughter to fill in for her. I'd like to introduce, on the fiddle, Tracy Marshall."

The crowd applauded, except there were several in the audience who had apparently heard Tracy play the previous afternoon back at camp. They stood and started shouting.

"You go, Tracy!"

"All right, Tracy. Play it, girl!"

"Yay, Tracy. Woohoo!"

Everyone on stage started laughing as Tracy blushed. The audience loved those dimples and started laughing and applauding again.

"We're gonna kick things off with *Pike County Breakdown*," Trevor said into the microphone.

Then he started the fast instrumental tune with a quick banjo roll. Darcy and Dawn were standing back by the soundboard. The sound man, Jerry Williamson, stood over hundreds of tiny knobs, adjusting one from time to time, making sure the mix on stage was perfect. Jerry was a dear friend to almost all the musicians in bluegrass music, and certainly to those on stage. He was known for being one of the best sound engineers in the industry. He was also a great musician and songwriter himself. He leaned over and bumped Darcy's shoulder. "You done good, momma."

"I'm about to explode," Darcy said. "That little girl never ceases to amaze me."

The band went on to play several more songs. Tracy was clearly having the time of her life. You couldn't have chiseled the smile off of her face.

Then Trevor said, "I want to introduce my good friend and our guitar player, Ben Salinger, ladies and gentlemen. He's gonna sing a duet for you this afternoon with little Tracy. It's called *Sittin' On Top of the World*." Trevor looked out from the stage to find Darcy. He knew she would be near the soundboard. They finally locked eyes. "For you, sweetie," he said, pointing to her.

Again, Trevor kicked off the song with his banjo roll as Ben and Tracy sang. The audience clapped and yelled after every chorus. Ben smiled and looked over at Tracy while she sang harmony with him. When the song was over, the crowd jumped to their feet with a roaring ovation.

When the applause died down, a few faceless voices from the audience began to shout, "Do *Bonaparte's Retreat!*"

"Bonaparte's Retreat!"

"Yeah, Tracy. Bonaparte's Retreat!"

Ben leaned down to Tracy. "You wanna do it, kiddo?"

Tracy smiled and nodded. Ben gave Trevor a thumbs up. Trevor acknowledged them, and Ben took off his guitar and darted to the back of the stage to get Trevor's old banjo.

"Okay, folks," Trevor said. "Apparently, some of you have heard this. Tracy just learned this tune, and I think you'll enjoy it. We'll wrap our set up today with *Bonaparte's Retreat!*"

Again, the crowd erupted as Tracy stepped back from the microphone and quickly tuned her fiddle down to open D. She returned to the microphone with a few quick fine-tuning tweaks, and off she went. She knew Uncle Ben would be there and ready when it was his time to play.

Tracy played the opening phrases flawlessly, her foot tapping, her hips rocking to the beat. Her listeners stared in awe, heads bobbing up and down, hands patting knees, toes tapping under lawn chairs. Just as Tracy had anticipated, Ben walked up and started playing with her right on cue. The audience became completely silent as the breathtaking duet rang from the large speakers on each side of the stage, and echoed across the campground.

Dawn was spellbound, her mouth gaping open. Darcy put her arm around Dawn as she laughed and cried, her other hand over her mouth. "Oh, my God," she whispered, pulling Dawn tightly against her.

She knew she had made the right decision. The rest of the band was standing to the side of the stage, watching. They, too, knew something special was happening. Judy had tears running down her face as well. Trevor had both hands resting on top of his head, fingers clasped, his gaze locked on Tracy's every move. He broke his gaze occasionally only to look out at Darcy, at the audience, and then back at Tracy.

Darcy noticed Woody standing off to the side of the audience, near the front, arms folded, watching what was happening on stage and grinning with pride. "He never comes to the stage area," she thought.

She shook her head and refocused on the stage. When she knew the end of the tune was near, Darcy leaned down to Dawn. "Come on, let's go, sweetie." Then she turned to Jerry and said, "Thanks, Jer. I'll see you a bit later."

Darcy and Dawn made their way through the rows of music fans in lawn chairs in order to get to the side of the stage. The tune quickened as Tracy reached the final volley of the last phrase, her bow snapping back and forth, and her head snapping back and forth with it. Darcy and Dawn reached the back stage area just as Ben frailed his last chord and Tracy ended on a long slow pull. The audience jumped to their feet with a deafening standing ovation— so much screaming and shouting.

"Tracy! Tracy! Tracy!"

"Thank you. Thank you," Tracy said repeatedly in her microphone, but it was barely audible. She smiled and walked over to Ben. He was laughing with tears in his eyes. Ben slid the banjo around behind him and reached down to hug her.

"Baby girl," he said. "That was amazing."

"Thanks, Uncle Ben. I feel like God was helping me. Do you think he was here, Uncle Ben?"

"I know he was, sweetie. I know he was. Look, your mom and Dawn are over there."

Tracy quickly walked off stage, stopping only for a moment to hug her dad. She pranced down the steps, and as soon as she reached Dawn, they embraced, jumping up and down, squealing like banshees. Darcy was clapping with joy, seeing her two little girls so excited. They both turned to her and locked their arms around each side of her waist.

"Mr. Woody!" Tracy shrieked as she saw him approach their little celebration. She ran to him and threw her arms around his waist. "Mr. Woody!"

"Hi there, munchkin. You did a great job, my dear. You really did."

Darcy walked over to them. "Hey, Woody. I saw you watching. You never leave your booth. What's up?"

"Oh, I wouldn't have missed this for the world. When I heard her playing with the band, I rushed right over. Honey, what you've done with her is unbelievable."

"Well, these days, Woody, I think it's more between her and God. I've never seen such passion in a child. I'm glad you came over. She loves you to pieces, ya know."

"Well," Woody said, shaking his head with a smile, watching Tracy run back to her sister. He left it at that.

"Hey Woody, have you seen Preacher Stan?" Darcy said.

"Yes, he was sitting back there with Doc, listening to your baby rock the world."

"Oh, I see them. I'll catch up with you later, Woody. Thanks again for coming over."

Darcy gave Woody a hug, and walked around the rows of chairs to get to Stan and Doc. The stage hands were setting up for the next band, so Jerry was just playing recorded music through the P.A. System. Most of the crowd were scattering, some heading to the vendor area, others back to their camps. Stan and Doc hadn't moved. When Darcy approached them, they were in a pretty involved conversation.

"Well, hey there," Stan said as she walked up to them. He and Doc stood up, and Stan wrapped his arms around Darcy. Then Doc gave her a hug

"Hi, Darcy," Doc said. "That little girl of yours is incredible."

Darcy grabbed a lawn chair that was in front of them, spun it around, and sat down facing the two. "Thanks Doc. But I don't think it's me anymore. This is like a thing between her and God, and what's so neat is that she knows it. She has such a beautiful relationship with God, it warms my heart. She has always been such a gentle spirit, just like Mary Alice, but this is blowing me away."

Both of the men looked mesmerized as they stared at Darcy's glowing face, listening to her report. "That's great," Stan said. "She's a special little girl, that's for sure. But how is Trevor taking it? Her relationship with God, I mean."

"He's not buying it, of course. He's excited and all, and he loves both of those girls with everything he's got. But he just keeps telling me what a good job I'm doing and that her gift is just something that some kids are lucky enough to have. He doesn't want to hear anything about God. If he sees Tracy reading her Bible or walks in on me praying with the girls, he'll just leave the room. He doesn't say bad things about God—he just won't acknowledge Him."

Darcy was trying hard to hold back her tears. Stan leaned forward and took both of her hands in his. "Sweetie, you and the girls are giving him the best example you can. I'm sure God is working on his heart, and he'll just have to come around in his own time and on his own terms."

"Just don't let it chisel away at your own faith," Doc said. "Stay strong, and Trevor will no doubt see that strength."

The three spoke for a few minutes more and then leaned down into a huddle, wrapping their arms around each other while Stan said a prayer.

Trevor gathered up his banjos and had Tracy's fiddle case hanging over his shoulder when he walked away from the stage area, glancing over and seeing Darcy with Stan and Doc. He shook his head and glanced back at Tracy and Dawn. "Come on, girls, let's head back to camp. I'm hungry. How 'bout you?"

"Yeah! Let's eat!" they shouted.

Ben and Kevin picked up their instruments and followed close behind.

"I'll see you guys over there a little later," Judy said. "I want to go check in on Tom."

Tracy got to play two more times on stage with the band that weekend and made many new friends and fans. The band all agreed that if Darcy wanted Tracy to be their fiddler, they would respect her wishes. Darcy was having the time of her life just watching Tracy grow on stage. She scarcely even thought about Weiser. But, while Darcy was watching Tracy, Judy was watching Darcy.

Later that year, in October, the group gathered again in Athens, Alabama, for the Tennessee Valley Old Time Fiddlers Convention. The band would compete again, and so would Darcy. But this time, Tracy would do what she had worked so hard for. She was going to compete in the Apprentice Division. She and Dawn could hardly contain their excitement. They had been coming to this festival their entire lives. For them, it was a magical place. A place where music was everything.

Tracy often wondered if this is what heaven would be like. Darcy spoke to them often about Weiser, Idaho, and her dream of being there some day. But the girls couldn't imagine how anything could be bigger or better, or more magical than Athens.

On Friday night, all the usual preliminaries, jamming, and catching up with old friends filled the evening. Judy, Ben, and Kevin hung out at Trevor and Darcy's campsite in the parking lot most of the time. They talked and practiced their tunes. Again, like clockwork, Jack Hanford and his band walked by the camp, eyeing things.

"We're going to get it again this year!" he shouted, smiling, but failing at his attempt to appear like he was joking.

"Whatever, Jack," Ben said, while the rest shook their heads.

Late Friday evening, it was getting cool, and the instruments were all in their cases. The group sat around outside, drinking hot chocolate and talking about days past. It was a calm, quiet evening. Darcy thought the girls had settled in, but the quiet came to a screeching halt when she heard Tracy and Dawn running inside the motorhome. They came crashing out of the door and down the steps.

"Mom...Mom," Tracy shouted, running up to Darcy with a piece of paper in her hand. Dawn was close behind her but seemed a little more reserved, almost embarrassed.

"Mom, Dawn wrote a poem!" Tracy panted, out of breath.

"Really?" Darcy said. "You wrote a poem? Nice work, honey. Let's hear it."

"No. It's nothing, really. You don't want to hear it," Dawn said.

"It's so cool, sis. You should read it," Tracy said.

"We'd love to hear it," Judy said.

After a few minutes of coaxing, Dawn finally agreed to share her poem. There weren't any lawn chairs left so she sat on Kevin's knee. "So, what's it called?" Kevin asked, patting her on the back.

"I think I'm just going to call it *Sisters*."

Darcy smiled. Her heart melted just at the sound of the title.

"Go on, sweetie, that sounds really good," Trevor said.

Dawn grabbed the paper out of Tracy's hand, squinting at her. "Thanks," She said, as sarcastically as she could.

"Okay," she began. "Sisters."

"Today as I walk through this dream we call life,
I think of the one with the blister.
Though her gift is so big, she never forgets,
there is no tighter tie than a sister.

We dance and we sing, we share everything.
We fight, though the win so clearly with her.
She laughs and reminds me of her other family,
yet there's no tighter tie than a sister

She's one year older, my hero I'd say.
I'd do anything to assist her.
Her music so dear, and God is so near.
But there's no tighter tie than a sister.

She never lets others get in between us.
When smiling, no one can resist her.
I'm never alone in this world, 'cause you know,
There's no tighter tie than a sister."

Dawn was finished, but a hush hung over the camp. Dawn looked around at everyone staring back at her. "What?" she said.

Finally, they all started clapping. "Honey, that was beautiful," Darcy said.

Kevin wrapped his arms around her in a bear hug from behind. "Baby girl, that was incredible," he said.

Dawn squirmed her way loose from Kevin to hug her mom. Her shyness and embarrassment faded away and her face lit up.

"Wasn't that cool?" Tracy said. "That was so cool."

As the girls retreated back into the motorhome, Judy leaned over to Darcy. "Well, if you were ever worried about sibling rivalry, I think you can forget it," she said.

Darcy looked back at Judy with tears welling up in her eyes. "I'm truly blessed."

Saturday is always a busy day at the Athens Fiddlers Convention. The crowds gathered from all over the area, musicians jamming everywhere, competitions on stage, and judges hard at work sifting through unimaginable talent. When it was time for the blue-grass band competition, Fiddler's Roost made the familiar march through the Founders Hall reception area, out to the makeshift stage on the huge front porch. This time, not only was Tracy there in the band, but Darcy was there too.

"Ladies and gentlemen, Fiddler's Roost is next and will be starting things off with a favorite by Bob Wills, *Faded Love.*"

Fiddlers had all but stopped playing *Faded Love* at Athens in competition because it was so overdone as a fiddle tune, but Trevor thought the judges and fans might like to hear the full song. He looked across the stage and nodded at Darcy. Darcy in turn looked over at Tracy. "Ready, hon?"

Tracy nodded, and they kicked off with a fiddle intro. The band joined in, and the girls must have played the sweetest and purest twin-fiddle adaptation of *Faded Love* the crowd had ever heard. When the band came around to the first verse, Trevor started singing the lyrics in his best, not so obvious, Bob Wills impression. "As I look at the letters that you wrote to me, it's you that I am thinkin' of..."

The crowd sat mesmerized, everyone smiling, many tapping their feet. Darcy and Tracy played another twin fiddle break in the middle of the song. Darcy was completely focused on her playing, but stared into the crowd as if she were playing for one particular person. She would play for one, then shift her gaze and play for another. This was her remarkable gift for engaging the audience in her music. But Tracy, on the other hand, was staring at her mom. She was so proud and excited to be standing on stage and playing with her hero. What a magical time this was for her.

The song ended with loud applause, yelps, and whistles from the audience. The band followed up the song with an instrumental number called *Train 45*. It was about as fast a tune as was ever played on that stage, and highlighted Trevor's banjo prowess when he kicked it off. Once again, the real highlight of the tune was watching Darcy and Tracy play a twin fiddle break. But this time, the two fiddlers were facing each other, pushing each other on to more and more complicated riffs as their bows were bouncing and rosin dust was clouding up around them. It was such a glorious spectacle that even those playing on stage enjoyed it, huge grins on their faces as they kept time. Even the emcee was smiling as he bounced up and down while sitting at his table at the end of the porch.

As soon as the last beat was played, the crowd jumped to their feet and cheered. Darcy and Tracy, both still facing each other, lifted their bows and fiddles straight into the air in victory. They laughed and embraced in a long rocking hug.

"Fiddler's Roost, everybody!" the emcee shouted as the band filed off of the stage, back into the front door.

It just so happened that Buckeye Bluegrass was next and were waiting inside the foyer. Jack was first in line and caught Darcy's attention as she walked by. "Nice job. You got some help, I see," he said.

Darcy did her best to ignore it, but inside, she was fuming as they walked down the steps in back of the hall. "Doesn't that guy ever give up?" Darcy asked.

Trevor was walking in front of her and was the only one that heard her. They walked through the crowd of musicians in the back of the building, many congratulating them and even some applause was heard.

"Nicely done, you guys," someone yelled from the crowd.

"That was awesome, you guys," Kevin said to Darcy and Tracy as they cleared the crowds and headed back to camp. "You two were smokin' it!"

Everyone laughed and kept walking. Trevor put an arm around Tracy, his other hand holding his banjo to his side. "I am so proud of you guys. That was incredible."

Dawn came running from the front of the building where the audience was. Woody was close behind her, unable to keep up. He smiled, walking as fast as he could. As soon as Dawn caught up to Tracy they held hands and started jumping up and down together, squealing at the top of their lungs. "That was so cool!"

Dawn squealed. "You should have heard everyone out there. They loved it."

"That's good, that's good," Darcy said, laughing. "But settle down before you break something."

They had all calmed down and caught their breath by the time they reached the motorhome and started packing their instruments back into the cases. Kevin put his bass inside.

"I think I'm going to go walk around the vendor area and see what else is going on," Ben said.

"I'll join you," Kevin said.

"Me too," Judy said. "I saw a bunch of jewelry tables up there."

Ben and Kevin both rolled their eyes and started to walk away.

"Shut up," Judy said as she caught up with them. They all walked away laughing.

Tracy and Dawn went inside and disappeared to the back bedroom. Trevor and Darcy sat alone out front, catching their breath and taking it all in. Not a word—just smiles. After a few minutes, Tracy walked out of the motorhome and down the steps with a serious look on her face.

"What is it, sweetie?" Darcy said.

"Mom...when I got off the stage, I started thinking about Grandma B." That's what she called Gladys Bartlett, Mary Alice's mom.

"Really? That's nice, honey. Why do you think that is?"

"I don't know," Tracy said.

"Do you want to go visit her when we get back?"

"Yeah, I think I do."

Tracy had seen her natural grandmother several times throughout her life. Darcy would often stop by to visit her with the girls after church on Sundays. Mary Alice and Wendy were never there. Tracy had never met Mary Alice but still referred to her as Mother. Darcy was Mom—Mary Alice was Mother. Tracy had also never met her other sister, Wendy.

"Yes, we'll do that next Sunday," Darcy said. "It'll be fun."

CHAPTER 6

Restoration

"You don't choose your family.
They are God's gift to you, as you are to them."
~ Desmond Tutu

Later that afternoon at Athens, when it was time for the fiddle competition in the Apprentice Category, young kids began lining up behind Founders Hall. Some of them were still jamming with friends and parents, but many were standing in silence, nervously waiting for their name to be called. Tracy was tuning her fiddle while surrounded by the entire band.

"It's going to be fine, Tracy," Kevin said, looking around at the other kids.

"Yes it is," Darcy said with a glare aimed at Kevin, her piercing eyes and scolding forehead notifying him to put a lid on it.

"Are you sure you can't play the banjo with me, Uncle Ben?" Tracy asked.

"Not this time, sweetie. We don't want to distract the judges from the fiddle playing," he said.

"Daddy, are you sure *Shannon Waltz* will be okay for the second tune?"

"It'll be fine, Tracy. You need to breathe, baby girl," Trevor said.

"Okay, the next two," the volunteer said, motioning to Tracy and the young boy behind her.

Dawn gave Tracy a hug but didn't say a word.

"You guys break a leg. Blow 'em away, Tracy," Judy said.

Trevor and Tracy walked up the back steps into the back door. Darcy, Dawn, Judy, Ben, and Kevin left the crowd of little people to make their way around the building to the front where they heard one of the contestants scratching out a tune as best she could. When she was finished, the crowd gave her a polite applause for effort. Darcy saw Woody standing in the back of the seating area under a tree near the soundboard, so she led the others in that direction.

When they arrived, Darcy smiled at Woody and asked, "Are you standing here watching all the fiddles you built compete with each other?"

"Oh, I suppose," he said with a grin.

The group waited nervously as the few kids that were ahead of Tracy played their best two tunes for the judges. The crowd continued their polite applause, wanting to encourage the students to keep doing better for next year. Then it was time. "Ladies and gentlemen, our next contestant is Tracy Marshall. Judges, Tracy Marshall. *Bonaparte's Retreat* and *Shannon Waltz*. Contestant number fourteen, Tracy Marshall."

With the same polite applause, Trevor and Tracy took to the stage and walked up to the two microphones in the middle. The stagehands made a few quick adjustments to the microphone stands, and then Trevor gave Ben's guitar a gentle strum to make sure it was still in tune. Likewise, Tracy quickly tapped each of the fiddle strings with her bow, then looked over and nodded to her daddy.

"Don't forget to breathe," he said, softly enough not to be picked up by his microphone. Tracy knew her daddy was trying to get her to smile and relax. It worked. At that instant, she smiled at him and the crowd disappeared. It was just her and her daddy.

She kicked off *Bonaparte's Retreat*. Trevor accompanied her lightly. He knew he didn't have to be there because that particular tune is capable of carrying itself, especially for her. But he wanted to be there for his little girl. And besides, her next tune was a waltz, which would most certainly need his backup.

Tracy executed the tune with perfection. Her double stops rang throughout the college campus and everyone from the audience to the vendors to the clueless folks in their campers were quiet—spellbound. It was like time stood still for Tracy, so that she could show her daddy what she could do.

Tracy glanced up and saw her mom standing in the back with both hands over her mouth. But she couldn't see the tears running down Darcy's face. Just like Lexington, when Tracy played the last phrase of quick notes into the finale, the audience jumped to their feet with whistles and shouts, cheering with hands over their heads. Tracy smiled at her daddy until she realized that all these people were cheering for her. She turned and looked at them in amazement.

"Okay, okay," the emcee said. "Have a seat. She's not done yet." He laughed.

The judges were smiling but motioned at the emcee to keep things moving. Once everyone quieted down, the emcee turned and looked at Tracy with an encouraging smile. "Go ahead, honey, whenever you're ready." He walked to the side of the porch.

Tracy played her pickup notes and Trevor joined in her rendition of *Shannon Waltz*. It was so much slower than her first tune, but it was soothing after what the audience had been listening to all morning. This time, Tracy was able to play to the audience with her signature dimpled smile.

When she finished, the crowd stood in applause once again, but this time, with a little more composure, like a real sense of respect. All of the judges were smiling and shaking their heads in amazement, but they didn't stand.

The Marshalls left Athens that year with three trophies and a poem. Traveling up Interstate 65, the Marshall family sang songs almost all the way home, Trevor continuously starting another one that they hadn't done in years. The girls tried to keep up. On the large dashboard, there were trophies for Second Place Bluegrass Band, First Place Junior Fiddler, and First Place Apprentice Fiddler. Laid next to them was a neatly folded piece of paper—Dawn's poem.

After they dropped Judy off at her house, they continued up I-65 to Bowling Green, and across the Cumberland Mountains toward home, near Prestonsburg, where they spent a quiet, restful week recharging their batteries.

Sunday morning rolled around and the family was getting ready for church. "Do you still want to go see Grandma B this afternoon?" Darcy asked Tracy.

"Yeah, Mom. Can we please?"

"Yes, I spoke to her on the phone yesterday and they're looking forward to our visit. You sure you don't want to go to church with us, Trev?"

"Oh, I'm pretty sure," Trevor said. "You know better."

"I know, I know. I just wish you would consider it sometime."

After church, Darcy and the girls stopped to greet Preacher Dave on their way down the steps. "Nice message today, Dave. Thanks," Darcy said.

"Well, well, look who we have here," Dave said, leaning over to greet the girls. He looked back at Darcy, smiling a little less. "How is that husband of yours?" he asked.

"He's doing just fine, Dave."

"You need to get him in here."

"I know, Dave, I know. Have a good day now," Darcy said as she turned, shook her head, and motioned for the two girls to keep moving down the steps.

When the three arrived at Bob and Gladys's house, Gladys was standing in the doorway waiting for them. She waved and went out to greet them as they pulled in the driveway. "Hey there, girls!" she shouted.

"Hi," Darcy said. "How are you guys doing?"

"We're all fine. Come on in. Are you all hungry?"

"Oh no. We're fine. I have dinner waiting at home."

"Well, okay. Come in and have a seat. Come over here and let me see you," Gladys said, opening her arms to Tracy. "My goodness, you're all grown up."

Tracy sat in Gladys's lap, though she was far too big to do it comfortably. That was just where she always went when they visited. They chatted for a while and Tracy told Gladys all about her win at Athens the week before. "Dawn wrote a really cool poem while we were there," Tracy told Gladys.

"When is Tracy going to meet her other sister?" Dawn asked, quickly changing the subject. "I keep hearing about this other sister."

"Well, Dawn!" Darcy glared, then quickly turned to Tracy. An awkward silence fell over the room.

"Well, hello there," Bob said as he walked into the living room with a tray of brownies in one hand and a pitcher of milk and glasses in the other.

"Hi, Mister Bob," Darcy said. She got up from her chair and gave him a hug after he set everything on the coffee table. Dawn still had a look of confusion on her face and kept looking between Tracy and her mom. Bob looked around at the awkward faces as the room went silent again.

"What in the world did I walk into?" he said, giggling.

"I think I'd like to meet my mother eventually," Tracy said. "But I'd like to meet my big sister real soon, if that's okay."

"Well, honey, I think that would be fine if it's okay with your mom," Gladys said, looking at Darcy. "I can give Mary Alice a call."

"I think that would be great," Darcy said. "But this is the first I've heard of it. Girls, let's go home and talk to daddy about it first. I'm sure it'll be just fine."

After a few brownies and some milk, mixed with a lot of chatter, Darcy and the girls loaded into the car to head home. "You can give Mary Alice a call if you like, Gladys, to let her know what's going on. I'll call you tonight just to firm things up," Darcy said.

The following Saturday, Darcy drove Tracy back over to Bob and Gladys's house where Wendy was waiting for them. Dawn stayed home for an afternoon daddy-date. Wendy had only learned of her sister the year before and was never really sure what to do about it, if anything. Wendy had been dealing with a lot during that time in her life while just learning about her father and then her sister. She was only sixteen herself, so it was a lot to take in. She sat at her Mamaw's house, excitedly waiting to meet her sister.

Darcy and Tracy walked into the living room where Wendy sat on the loveseat—the exact spot Mary Alice was sitting when she and Darcy held hands and agreed to the adoption. Tracy walked across the room and sat next to her. They both smiled and stared at each. Darcy could barely contain her tears. Even though Tracy was three years younger than Wendy, these girls were obviously sisters, all the way down to the dimples.

Tracy reached for her big sister's hand. "Hi. I'm Tracy."

"I know. I'm Wendy."

"I know."

The two continued to stare at each other. They too felt like they were looking into a mirror.

"Do you have any other brothers or sisters?" Tracy asked.

"Two little brothers. You?"

"I have another sister. She's a year younger."

"What do you like to do?" Wendy asked.

"Well, I love to read and I love school and church. But mostly I love to play my fiddle."

"Fiddle?"

"Yeah. You know, a violin. What do you like to do?"

"I love sports. Mostly softball. But I'm going to be a nurse."

"Wow! That's cool," Tracy said.

"You want to go meet some of my friends?" Wendy asked. "They're waiting for me."

Tracy's eyes lit up. "You drive?"

"Sure."

Tracy turned to Darcy. "Can I, Mom?"

Darcy looked at Gladys with a questionable grin.

"Oh, she's a good driver," Gladys assured her.

"Can you just take her to our house, honey, when you're done?" Darcy said, looking at Wendy with a smile.

"Yes, ma'am."

"Well, don't be gone too long or you'll miss hamburgers," Darcy said. "Wendy, you're welcome to join us for supper if you like."

The girls ran through the door, out to the street, and jumped into Wendy's car.

"Well, that was pretty amazing," Darcy said, shaking her head.

"Glad that's done," Bob said as he stood from his chair, watching through the big picture window as the girls drove out of sight.

"I'll leave you ladies. I have a project in the basement to tend to."

"Okay, Bob. It was good to see you," Darcy said.

"You too, hon."

Tracy and Wendy got to know each other quite well over the next few years. Tracy played her fiddle for Wendy on occasion and sometimes went to watch Wendy play softball. Dawn really liked Wendy too, but it was usually just Tracy and Wendy on the outings.

A few weeks went by. Tracy and Wendy were having lunch at the chili parlor where Wendy worked, and where they usually gathered with their friends.

"Hey, do you want to meet my mom?" Wendy asked as Tracy was taking a bite of her chili.

Tracy coughed, trying to get her chili down to catch her breath. She reached for the pop in front of her and washed everything down without incident. "Really?"

"Yeah. We've been talking about it and I think she'd like to meet you."

"I'd love to. I better mention it to my Mom first, though."

When Wendy dropped Tracy off at her house, Tracy went straight to the music room where Darcy was practicing a new piece she was learning on her fiddle. Tracy quietly leaned on the door frame, listening intently until the tune was over. "Wow! What was that?" Tracy asked.

"Oh, hey there. I didn't hear you come in. It's just something I've been working on. No big deal really"

"Well, it's beautiful. That's for sure."

"Thanks, sweetie. What's up?"

"Where's Daddy?"

"Oh, he's out back working on that motorhome."

"Oh." Tracy entered the music room and sat on a chair facing her mom.

"Everything okay?" Darcy asked.

"Yeah, I think so. Wendy just asked me if I wanted to meet her mom."

"Really!"

"Yeah."

"And how do you feel about that?" Darcy asked.

"Well, I've always wanted to meet her, but I can imagine this has all been really hard on her. I just don't want to upset her or anything."

"Sweetie, Mary Alice is a grown woman. I'm sure she knows if she's ready or not. She'll be fine."

"I suppose."

"She loves you, ya know."

"I know."

"You aren't mad at her, are you?" Darcy asked.

"Oh no. Nothing like that."

"Well, then. Maybe it's just time, honey."

"I guess it is."

It was a Saturday afternoon and Mary Alice was in the midst of preparing a taco supper for her family. In addition to Wendy, she now had two sons, Steve and Robby, with her husband, Darrell. She was in the middle of slicing tomatoes when the phone rang. She quickly laid the knife aside and wiped her hands on the apron she was wearing. She picked the phone up. "Hello."

"Hello, Mother? This is Tracy."

Mary Alice was stunned at first, but gathered her thoughts quickly. "Well, hello there," she said. She pulled a chair out and sat at the dining table. "How are you?" Such a simple question that ran so deep in all directions.

"I'm fine. Is it okay if I call you Mother?" Tracy asked.

"Of course it is, honey. I would like that. Is everything okay?"

"Oh yes. Everything is great. I told Wendy I was going to call you. I guess she didn't mention it."

"Well, unfortunately, Wendy and I don't talk a lot these days. Have you two been having a good time together?"

"Yes. It's been a blast meeting her friends and hanging out. I don't know that I've ever eaten so much chili."

"Oh I know," Mary Alice laughed. "They do love their chili."

The phone fell silent for several seconds before Tracy finally said, "Mother, I just wanted you to know I don't have any bad feelings about all this or toward you."

Mary Alice paused and tears welled up in her eyes. "Well, what a mature thing to say. I'm so proud of you. I'm sure thankful for that, honey. And I want you to know it was the most difficult decision I've ever made, but I couldn't have given you the life I wanted you to have while living with my parents and having no idea what my future was going to be like. Are you living a good life?"

"Oh yes. Mom and Daddy are great. School is going well. I love going to church and singing and painting, and especially playing my fiddle."

"You play the fiddle?"

"Yes I do, and I love it. Mom's been teaching me for as long as I can remember. I won a big fiddle contest down in Athens, Alabama."

"Wow! How exciting. How are your folks doing?"

"They're doing really well," Tracy said.

"I'm glad. That's good to hear."

"Mother, is it okay if I come visit? I'd really like to meet you and my brothers."

Again, Mary Alice was stunned, but then smiled. "Sure, honey. Do you want to come now? You can join us for tacos."

"I would love that."

"Wendy will be back from the store shortly, and I'll have her come pick you up."

"Okay then. I'll see you when I get there."

After Tracy hung up the phone, she walked back into the music room where Darcy was reading and Trevor was looking through a song book.

"Hi, sweetie," Darcy said, looking up from her Bible. "What are you smiling so big about?"

"Where's Dawn?" Tracy asked.

"Oh, she's down at Rita's house, studying. What's up?"

"I just got off the phone with Mother and she invited me over for supper."

"Mother?" Trevor said.

"Mary Alice," Darcy explained.

"Oh."

"That sounds exciting, sweetie. Are you going?" Darcy asked.

"Yes. If it's okay with you guys. Wendy is coming to pick me up. I'm a little nervous. I get to meet my brothers too. Do you think they'll like me?"

Darcy chuckled. "They're going to love you, sweetie. I promise."

"Honey, don't forget we have that gig coming up next Saturday in Nashville," Trevor said.

"Okay, Daddy. I'll be ready."

When Wendy and Tracy walked in the front door, Mary Alice was dumbfounded. They were both smiling and their dimples were a perfectly matched set. Even with black hair on one and blonde on the other, there would be no question in anyone's mind that these two were sisters.

"Dang," Steve said. Robby simply stared.

Tracy didn't stop walking until she landed in the arms of Mary Alice. They were both crying by the time they were firmly embraced.

"You're so beautiful," Mary Alice said, trying to choke back the tears.

Wendy was still smiling, as if she had just brought her mom a really special gift.

"Well, these are your brothers," Mary Alice said, gesturing to her sons while wiping her face.

"Hi," Tracy said.

"Hi, I'm Steve. I'm ten."

"Hi, I'm Robby. I'm eight."

"I'm glad to finally meet you," Tracy said. She turned back to Mary Alice. "It smells really good in here."

"Well, let's go eat. Are you hungry?"

"I'm starved."

They all went in to the kitchen where Mary Alice had lined up plates and bowls of all the taco shells and toppings. They insisted that Tracy go through the line first. She nervously obliged. The two little boys were so taken by the sister they had only recently learned about, they couldn't help but stare. Wendy felt bad about it but didn't want to cause a scene.

After a nice long visit, Wendy and Tracy headed back to the car for the trip back home.

"I'm so full," Tracy said as she got out of Wendy's car. "Dinner was so much fun with you guys. I never really knew how I would feel, but now I know I'm completely comfortable around them. I really love your family," Tracy said.

"Well, they're your family too, and they love you," Wendy said.

Tracy closed the car door and leaned against it with her face in the open window. The girls chatted for several more minutes, replaying the evening and how much fun they had. "Good night, and thanks for the ride," Tracy said, finally ending the long conversation.

"Good night, sis. I'll give you a call tomorrow."

When Tracy got inside the house, she heard music coming from the music room. She stuck her head in the door and saw Darcy playing fiddle, with Trevor on guitar and Judy playing her mandolin. Dawn was sitting in the corner writing in her notebook.

"Aunt Judy!" Tracy shouted as she darted across the room. The tune they were playing fizzled to a halt as Judy put her mandolin aside to stand and hug Tracy. "What are you doing here?" Tracy asked.

"I had to come in for a week for a photography shoot. I'm shooting a horse farm down near Pikeville. I wasn't about to be in the area without my mandolin. How are you doing, sweetie?"

"Great! I just spent the evening with my mother, my other sister, and two brothers."

"Really!"

"It was so much fun."

Trevor smiled at Darcy. "I think we need some snacks."

"Tracy, come in the kitchen and help me with some soft drinks and chips," Darcy said as she walked out the door.

"Can I help?" Dawn asked.

"Yes, please," Darcy said. She put her arm around Tracy's shoulder as they left the room, Dawn following close behind. As soon as they got into the kitchen, Dawn leapt up on the countertop as Tracy went to the refrigerator for ice.

"So... how was it?" Darcy asked.

"It was so much fun, Mom. Mother made tacos for supper and they were really good."

"Just tacos?" Darcy said.

"No. She made beans and rice, too. Mom, they were so nice. Robby, the littlest brother didn't say much but he was funny. So was Steve."

"How is Mary Alice doing?"

"She seems to be doing great. I think she likes me."

"Sweetie, I told you, she loves you. They all do. You are family after all."

Tracy turned to Dawn. "So, you better be nice to me. I have another sister and two brothers."

Dawn grabbed a wet dish towel that was on the counter and threw it in Tracy's face. *Splat!*

Darcy's jaw dropped, and she started laughing.

"No, you didn't," Tracy yelled, reaching for the towel on the floor.

Dawn jumped down from the counter and ran, laughing, around the other side of the island, ducking her head. "No!" she screamed.

Tracy ran around the other side and threw the towel back at her while Darcy grabbed the two large pop bottles and slid to the corner of the kitchen, out of the way. She was laughing at all the pandemonium. The girls continued to scream and laugh and throw the towel at each other until Trevor and Judy walked in. Everyone froze.

"What in the world?" Trevor said as he looked around assessing the room. He smiled at Darcy. "Are you okay in here alone with these two?"

Tracy and Dawn had stopped and were staring at their dad with such a goofy look on their faces, Judy burst out laughing. She laughed so hard, she bent over with her hands on her knees. Trevor and Darcy followed suit, then the two girls joined in and completely lost it. They all had tears running down their faces.

Finally, Darcy caught her breath. "You guys grab this stuff," she said, motioning to Trevor and Judy to help her with the bowl of chips, glasses of ice, and the pop. "You girls clean this mess up."

The two continued to laugh as Dawn reached into the pantry for the mop while the adults returned to the music room. After several minutes of enjoying the snacks and chatting, Dawn ran in.

"Mom, Tracy's nose is bleeding."

"Oh, Lord," Darcy said. She was smiling. Not too worried, but she got up from her chair. "Let me see." They both went back into the kitchen to find Tracy leaning over the sink with a blood-soaked paper towel held to her nose.

"What happened?" Darcy asked.

"Nothing really," Dawn said. "I was mopping and she was just standing over here waiting for me to get done."

"It's okay, Mom," Tracy said. "It's just a nosebleed."

"Here, hold your head back," Darcy said. "But keep that on there."

After several minutes, the bleeding stopped, and the three of them went back to the music room. "Everything okay?" Trevor asked.

"I'm fine, Daddy. It was just a nosebleed. Mind if I jam with you guys?"

"Not at all. Break it out, baby girl," Judy said.

Tracy reached for her fiddle case and Dawn returned to the corner with her notebook and started writing. Nobody really knew what she was writing most of the time. The others brushed the chip crumbs from their hands and took one more drink from their glasses before they picked up their instruments and started tuning. It wasn't a school night, so the family stayed up late, visiting with Judy and playing music. Judy left to go back to her hotel room around midnight. She never liked imposing on the family for sleeping quarters, much to everyone's disappointment.

Darcy woke up early the next morning to the familiar smell of the coffee Trevor was making in the kitchen. "Good morning," she said as she walked in.

"Good morning, sleepyhead. Your cup is there on the counter."

"Thanks. You haven't heard anything out of the girls yet?"

"Not yet," Trevor said. "I think they were up talking long after we went to bed."

"Great. I'll go check on them."

First, Darcy opened Dawn's door slowly and peaked in. She was sound asleep. Then Darcy opened Tracy's bedroom door and walked in. Tracy was sound asleep as well, facing the wall with her back toward the door. Darcy smiled, seeing how peacefully her babies were resting. But Tracy's t-shirt had slid up a little in the night, revealing her back. Darcy noticed a dark spot on Tracy's skin that she had never seen before. She walked over and sat on the edge of the bed. She lifted the shirt a little more and looked, then put her hand on Tracy's shoulder. "Tracy, honey."

Tracy rolled over and opened her eyes. "Hey, Mom. Good morning," she said in her groggy, cracking early-morning voice. "What's up?"

"Honey, how did you get all these bruises on your back?"

"Bruises?"

CHAPTER 7

Disappointment

"There's no tragedy in life like the death of a child.
Things never get back to the way they were."
~ Dwight D. Eisenhower

"As many of you know, Trevor and Darcy Marshall's daughter, Tracy, has been battling leukemia for the past three years," Dave Jenson said as he delivered the prayer requests during the Sunday morning service. "Sweet Tracy lost her battle this past Friday, and has gone home to be with the Lord she loved so dearly."

Darcy sat in the front pew with her arm around Dawn, both of them with red swollen eyes, cheeks, and noses rubbed pink with tissue. Dawn's head was leaning on Darcy's chest. She continued to weep on and off during the service. Trevor was sitting on Dawn's other side, holding her hand.

"Tracy's funeral service will be held here at the building on Wednesday afternoon at 2 PM. You're all invited to attend. It will be followed by a graveside service over in the cemetery here by the side yard."

Mary Alice was sitting on the other side of Darcy, holding her hand. Wendy, Steve, and Robby were all on the other side of Mary

Alice. Wendy had laid her head in Mary Alice's lap and was also weeping during the service.

When services were over, Dave led a prayer and dismissed the church. He then walked to the front pew to greet and console Trevor and Darcy as everyone stood.

"Preacher Dave, this is Mary Alice, Tracy's Mother, and her kids. You met her parents when they visited here before Tracy was born," Darcy said.

"Welcome to our church, Mary Alice. I'm so sorry for your loss. If you and your family need anything at all, I'm at your service." He made Mary Alice nervous, but she shook his hand.

"Thank you, sir," she said.

Dave left them to go to the front door to greet the other members as they left.

"Do you guys want to come to the house for a bite to eat?" Darcy asked.

"No thanks, Darcy. That's really sweet. But, I want to get Wendy back home so she can lie down."

"I understand."

Mary Alice took both of Darcy's hands in her own and looked at her swollen eyes. "Thank you for taking such good care of Tracy."

"Oh God," Darcy said. "Thank you for giving her to us and letting us raise her. She was an amazing young lady."

Then Darcy turned to Mary Alice's children. "I want to thank you guys for stepping up to have that bone marrow test. There was no question in Tracy's mind right then that you all loved her so much. And she really loved you all, too." Darcy looked back at Mary Alice. "And you, my friend, were a perfect match. I'm just so sorry the doctors decided it was too late—that she was too weak to do the transplant."

"I'm sorry, too," Mary Alice said as they embraced.

As Trevor, Darcy, and Dawn were leaving the church, Preacher Dave grabbed Trevor's arm to hold him back from the others. "The best thing you can do right now is keep her playing her music," Dave said. Trevor looked at him with a stern eye and nodded his head.

Nobody said a word during the ride home. Darcy broke the silence as soon as they entered the kitchen through the back door of the house. "Do you want something to eat, honey?" Darcy asked Dawn.

"No thanks, Mom. I'm not really hungry." Dawn headed straight upstairs to her bedroom and closed the door. Trevor and Darcy went into the living room. After several more minutes of silence, Darcy doubled over, putting her face into her hands, and wept uncontrollably. Trevor sat next to her on the couch and rubbed her back.

"What are we going to do?" Darcy said through the tears.

"We're going to put one foot in front of the other and keep moving." After a few minutes, Trevor stood up, and said, "Can I make you something to eat?"

"No, I might get something later."

"Okay, I'll be back here," he said, and he left to go into the music room. Trevor closed the door and sat on the couch. For ten minutes, he stared at Tracy's fiddle case standing in the corner. Hardly blinking, he dropped his head and began sobbing quietly.

After what seemed like an eternity for the Marshall family, Wednesday finally rolled around. They arrived at the church, making their way through an endless stream of cars. The parking lot was already nearly full. "Mom, what's going on?" Dawn asked as she looked out of the car windows in all directions.

"Oh, my God." Darcy said. "Surely all these people aren't here for Tracy."

"Apparently they are," Trevor said. He saw someone motioning him to pull his car up to the front of the church building. A spot had been reserved for them. When Trevor pulled the car in, Darcy saw Judy, Ben, and Kevin standing at the doorway. She covered her mouth and began to cry. Ben and Kevin immediately walked to the passenger side of the car—Ben opening Dawn's door and Kevin opening Darcy's.

"Hey, munchkin," Ben said to Dawn as she got out of the back seat and wrapped her arms around his waist.

Darcy got out, put her arms around Kevin's neck, and kissed him on the cheek. "Thank you so much for coming," she said. "I thought you were in New York for something. I can't believe you came all this way."

"There is no place I'd rather be right now," Kevin said.

Ben and Kevin closed the doors, and Ben turned to Darcy for a hug. "I am so sorry," he said, fighting back the tears.

"God just didn't want her to suffer anymore," Darcy said in a muffled voice, her face buried in Ben's neck.

Kevin put his arm around Dawn as they all walked toward the front of the church. Trevor rounded the car to shake everyone's hands. He smiled at each of them. Darcy and Dawn went straight into Judy's arms, and all three broke down and cried. Darcy couldn't hold back anymore, and she melted into the safety of Judy's arms. Others were trying to get to the door, but stopped and waited, some crying along with them, others looking down at the ground waiting patiently for Darcy to grieve.

Finally, Trevor opened the front door of the church building and put his arm around Dawn. "Come on, sweetie," he said. "Let's go on in and get seated."

As Dawn entered the church, Trevor patted Darcy on the back and she too went in. Judy kept an arm around Darcy as they both walked down the aisle to the front pew.

"We'll be sitting right behind you," Judy said as she let Darcy go so she could sit down.

But before Darcy could take her seat, she looked around to acknowledge many of those who had come. Then, a few rows back, she saw Woody, Doc, and Preacher Stan sitting together. They all looked and nodded. "Oh my God," Darcy said. She walked back as they stood to greet her. "I can't believe you guys came."

"There's no way we were going to miss being here for you guys," Woody said as he put his arms around Darcy. "I'm really sorry. That little girl of yours was so precious to all of us."

Doc and Stan hugged Darcy before sitting down. She rejoined Trevor at the front pew as he waved back at the three men. Then Darcy saw Bob and Gladys sitting with Mary Alice, Wendy, Steve, and Robby on the third row on the other side of the church. "Oh no," she said to Trevor. "That's not going to work."

She walked over to the Bartlett family. "Hey there," she said. "What are you guys doing way back here? I'd really like it if you would all sit up front with us."

"That's okay Darcy, honey, don't worry about it, Bob said. "We're fine here."

"No, no, no," she insisted. "You guys are family and you need to be up here with us."

"Well, okay," Bob said, and they all stood.

Darcy hugged each of them as they made their way out of the tight space between the pews. When Mary Alice made her way to the aisle, Darcy threw her arms around her and they wept together for several minutes. Then Darcy and Gladys repeated the same scene. They made their way to the front pew where Trevor and Dawn were. Trevor stood to greet them. He knew Darcy had created a ruckus, but he expected no less. He simply shrugged his shoulders.

Meanwhile, Preacher Dave had a few men bringing chairs from the fellowship hall to set up around the perimeter of the auditorium. By the time services began, all of those chairs were full and there was standing room only. Dave began, "Ladies and gentlemen, Tracy's family would like to thank you for joining them today for this celebration of her life. Please bow your heads with me as we pray." The painful process of laying Tracy to rest had finally begun. Almost all of Tracy's music friends, friends from school, and friends from church were there.

At the end of the service, the pallbearers carried Tracy's casket through the side doors of the church building and into the cemetery where her grave had been prepared. The crowd followed behind them. Darcy heard the shuffle of feet and an occasional hymnal being returned to the pew backs—otherwise, the place remained quiet. The Marshalls, the Bartletts, and Tracy's bandmates were all in a tight group walking slowly under the trees to the gravesite. Woody, Stan, and Doc, followed close behind.

"We thought it would be nice to play a song or two, but your pastor said we couldn't do it in this church," Judy said, leaning into Darcy.

"Really?" Darcy asked.

"But of course," Trevor said, obviously annoyed.

"I'm so sorry," Darcy said. "It would have been so beautiful. It is an a cappella church, but I thought they would allow it for a funeral. I know Tracy would have loved it."

Trevor shook his head and continued walking slowly, holding Darcy's hand. As soon as the family arrived at the gravesite and were seated under the big green canopy, Dave began another sermon to finally put Tracy to rest. When it was over, Dave thanked everyone for being there and the crowd began to disperse. Darcy motioned for those around her to gather in closer. "Hey, can you guys come to the house for something to eat and spend a little time with us?"

"Of course," Doc said. "I'd like that."

"We can't," Mary Alice said. "I really need to get my Mom and Daddy back home, and these kids are really tired."

Darcy looked at Wendy and then back at Mary Alice, shaking her head. She knew the pain that they must be feeling, especially Wendy, who had become such a close friend and sister to Tracy. Darcy smiled and rubbed Wendy's arm. "Go home and get some rest, okay?" Wendy nodded her head, looking at the ground. "You come and see me, okay? Don't be a stranger."

"Okay," Wendy said, continuing to stare at the ground.

"Sorry, I need to head back to the house too," Woody said. "You guys enjoy each other."

The others agreed to meet at the house and started toward the parking lot. "Fall in behind us," Trevor said.

Preacher Dave was standing near the edge of the parking lot, greeting everyone as they left. Darcy and Trevor accompanied him for several minutes, chatting and thanking those she could for being there for Tracy. The others stood nearby, waiting and remembering all the special times with Tracy. When the crowd had thinned, Darcy turned and hugged Dave. "Thank you so much. It was a beautiful service," she said.

"Well, you're quite welcome. She was such a lovely little girl. We all loved her. If you need anything, Darcy, anything at all, you just let me or one of the elders know. If you ever want to just talk, my door is always open."

"Thanks Dave," Darcy said.

"So, do you think you might be a regular around here?" Dave said, turning to Trevor.

"Uh...not likely," Trevor said. "I understand my friends over there asked you about playing and singing a couple songs, but you told them no."

"Well, Trevor," Dave said. "That just isn't something we do here."

Darcy stayed quiet and looked at the ground, but she squeezed Trevor's arm and put her head against him.

"I know. I know," Trevor said, shaking his head again and reaching out his hand to shake Dave's. They all walked toward their cars, preparing to leave.

"Unbelievable," Trevor said, loud enough for the group to hear.

"Honey, you knew it was going to be that way. Just let it go," Darcy said. "It was a nice service."

"It was," he said.

When they arrived at the house, Trevor pulled their car all the way back to the front of the garage. Trevor, Darcy, and Dawn got out of the car as Trevor motioned for the other drivers to come all the way in.

"Only real friends get to come in the back door," Darcy said with a chuckle, as they paraded into the kitchen. "I'm going to just let you guys help yourselves. There are drinks in the fridge, salsa and cheese dip in the door there, bowls there in that cabinet, glasses next to them, and a couple two-liter bottles of pop under the counter."

Darcy sat at the kitchen table, and Dawn walked straight up to her bedroom. Darcy watched Dawn until she was out of sight, and then she glanced at Trevor. He too had been watching Dawn. He turned to Darcy, shook his head, and they both continued on with the conversation. "Is everything okay?" Stan asked.

The kitchen got quiet. Darcy sighed and dropped her chin into her hand, elbow resting on the table. "She loved Tracy so much," Darcy said. "I just don't know what she's going to do. And I don't know what I can do to help her."

"Kids are resilient," Stan said. "She'll be okay."

"What about you?" Judy asked Darcy. "How are you?"

"I'm just getting through a minute at a time," Darcy said. "One minute I'm thinking how blessed I was to be given such a beautiful little girl, and the next minute I wonder how God could be so cruel to entrust me with such a beautiful gift only to grab it away from me. How could He do such a thing?"

"How's your church life?" Stan asked.

"Over the past year, since Tracy got really bad, it's been non-existent. I called the church office every now and then to make sure we were on the prayer list, but frankly that was about it."

"You really need to lean on your church now, sweetie," Stan said.

Trevor got up from the table and walked out of the kitchen.

Darcy dropped her gaze to the floor and shook her head. "He wants nothing to do with the church," she said. "I've tried to get him to go for years. I still invite him every now and then, but he just wants no part of it."

"Has he ever been a member of a church before?" Doc asked.

"I think he probably was a long time ago, Doc. I don't know what happened. He never talks about it," Darcy said.

"People get hurt by the church for a lot of reasons," Stan said. "It might be worth broaching the subject with him once you both have had time to heal. I did notice that he was pretty agitated when he heard the preacher wouldn't let these guys play today."

"Yeah. Anytime something looks even remotely like legalism to him, he wants to punch something," Darcy said.

"Well, there you have it," Stan said. "He at least has some foundation to recognize legalism."

They heard Trevor plucking on his banjo back in the music room. Ben and Kevin slid down off the countertop to join him.

"We talked about faith before we got married," Darcy said. "It was important for me that he believed in God, and he said he does. He just wanted nothing to do with the church."

"That's really not that uncommon these days," Doc said. "I've learned of a new class of Christian called *The Dones*, meaning they are *done* with organized religion. It's a pretty interesting phenomenon."

"Well, I won't bother him now," Stan said. "But if he ever wants to talk to another guy about it, feel free to send him my way."

"I will, Preacher Stan. I will."

"Do you want to play some music, sweetie?" Judy asked, putting her hand on Darcy's arm.

"I can't, Judy. I just can't." Darcy put her face in her hands and began to sob. Judy put her arms around her.

"This might be a good time for a prayer," Judy said, looking at Stan.

Stan and Doc walked over to the girls and put their arms around both of them while Stan said a prayer for comfort. When everyone said, "amen," Judy continued to rub Darcy's back and shoulders until Darcy was able to talk again. "You know, it scares me to death to think I may never be able to play again. When I pick up my fiddle, it's like picking up Tracy. Then I realize she's gone all over again. It was such a joy watching her play."

"I understand, sweetie," Judy said. "I do. But I know you enough to know that fiddle is as much a part of you as your heart.

In fact, I'm almost willing to say it is your heart." Everyone smiled, almost to the point of a chuckle.

"It just isn't important anymore," Darcy said.

Then they heard Ben and Kevin join in playing with Trevor. "I think they're getting a little serious in there," Doc said.

"Well, grab that stuff off the counter," Darcy said. "Let's go join them. I can still listen."

The four of them retired to the music room to join the others. Judy removed a mandolin from its hook on the wall and started jamming with them. Darcy sat in her usual chair and looked on. Trevor looked at her while he was playing, his eyes begging her to join them. She just smiled and shook her head no.

They played and visited for a while before Judy, apparently noticing that Trevor and Darcy were getting tired, stood and hung the mandolin back on the wall. "Hey, you guys," Judy said. "I need to get on the road. I have some work I need to get done at home."

"Yeah, we need to run, too," Stan said. "Doc has a plane to catch early tomorrow."

"Yep. Yep I do," Doc said.

All the hugs and the tears began again as the instruments were being put away and everyone picked up a bowl or a glass or a bag to carry back into the kitchen. "If you guys need anything, please just let us know," Judy said.

"That goes for all of us, my friend," Ben said as he squeezed Trevor's shoulder.

"Thank you so much for coming and spending some time with us," Darcy said. "You've given us a little light on an otherwise terrible day."

They smiled and filed out the back door and into their cars. When the last one had pulled out of the driveway and the back door was closed, Trevor and Darcy walked into the living room, sat down, and exhaled. The house was silent, until several minutes later when they heard Dawn's bedroom door open. She walked down the stairs and into the living room, plopped down on the couch, and laid her head on Darcy's lap, not saying a word. Darcy put her arm over her and stroked her hair. Silence hung over the house once again. Their day was done.

Weeks had passed and Darcy worked to try to get her family's life back in order. She cleared the house of all the medical supplies that had accumulated over the last three years. She never picked up her fiddle, but when she was home alone, she occasionally went into Tracy's bedroom and cried. Almost every day, Dawn came home from school and walked straight into her bedroom and closed the door. She came out only for supper on occasion, saying little, then went back in and closed the door. She always insisted that she had homework to do. Trevor became a workaholic, keeping long hours at the music store he managed. He told Darcy that he was inundated with new music students.

Darcy often walked into the music room and looked around as if trying to find something. She remembered the days when the room was filled with joy, when they played and sang with their friends as Dawn happily listened in the corner and wrote in her notebook. "Dawn," Darcy whispered to herself. "Poor, sweet Dawn." Tears filled her eyes as she looked around the room again, but this time in near panic. She went to the kitchen, picked up the phone, and called the church.

"Hi, Rhonda. Can I get in to see Preacher Dave? Okay, I'll be there shortly. Thanks."

After she arrived at the church, Darcy waited in a chair for several minutes outside the preacher's office until Rhonda, the church secretary, stuck her head through a sliding glass window. "Hi, Darcy. Preacher Dave is down in the conference room. They're just wrapping up an elders' meeting. He'll be with you in just a few minutes."

"Okay. Thanks, Rhonda." Darcy looked up when she heard the conference room door squeak open, echoing through the hallway. Dave motioned her to come down as he started walking toward her.

"Darcy, honey, would you prefer to meet with me in private, or is it okay if the elders join us?"

"They can join us. That's fine," she said, thinking all along that it was an odd question. But after she thought a second, she did have something she wanted to discuss with them anyway.

Dave opened the door for her and she walked into the conference room. The four elders stood, smiled, and greeted her.

"Have a seat here, Darcy," Dave said. "How are you doing? How's the family?"

"Well, that's what I wanted to talk to you about. I just feel like I need the prayers and the strength of the church, because I'm afraid I'm alienating them." She barely got the words out before she started crying. Her hands were shaking.

One of the elders slid a box of tissue in front of her without saying a word. "Thank you," Darcy said, taking one from the box.

The men quietly waited for her to regain her composure. "But before I get started, since we're all here," she said, "I want to try to understand something. I've been trying to figure out why you guys wouldn't let our friends play music at Tracy's funeral. She loved that music—and she loved our friends so much."

"Darcy, there's no way we could have allowed that to happen. Surely, you know that instruments in church are a sin," one of the elders said.

"What are you talking about? A sin? According to whom?" She felt her whole body tightening in anger. "You have the nerve to take what is so obviously a gift entrusted to so many people, including my little girl, and call it a sin?"

"There is no authority in the New Testament for instruments," another elder said.

"So, the fact that instruments and singing for the joy of the Lord in the Old Testament, means nothing to you guys? It's practically a commandment in the Psalms."

"But, that's the Old Testament. The only true church is the New Testament Church." Dave said.

"Huh?" Darcy's face twisted in confusion. "I may not be a Bible scholar, but you do know that teaching and admonishing one another with psalms, hymns, and spiritual songs, is mentioned more than once in the New Testament, right?"

"Songs, not instruments," an elder said.

"You know," Darcy reflected. "I thought a cappella singing was just something we traditionally do for Sunday morning worship. I love it. I really do. But I didn't know we were doing it because of some narrow minded edict from ignorant leaders. Gentlemen, psalms, by definition, are songs accompanied by an instrument. You guys have really lost sight of what we're supposed to be doing here. We're supposed to be inviting the lost into the Lord's church, not chasing them away. This isn't some kind of exclusive social club, you know." She restrained herself and looked back down at the table. "I'm sorry," she said. "I'll get to the real reason I'm here."

"Please do," one of the elders said, clearly annoyed by her outburst.

"Okay. Look, Trevor spends all hours at the store these days and poor Dawn is always closed up in her bedroom. We never talk anymore. I feel like I'm stuck in a well all by myself, and can't figure out a way to climb out of it."

The men continued to listen as Preacher Dave took notes on a yellow legal pad. Then Dave said, "You mentioned earlier that you thought you were alienating them. Why is that?"

"Well, I've been so depressed and in my own funk, I just don't think they want to be around me. I can't really blame them."

"Do you pray about it? Turn it over to God?" one of the elders asked.

"I have to be honest here, gentlemen. I haven't felt very close to God at all since Tracy died." The room fell silent except for Dave tapping his pencil on the pad of paper. After becoming un-nerved by the tapping, Darcy broke the silence. "Why would God let that happen? That's all I've been able to think about. Why would He do that?"

Dave looked around the room at each of the elders, and then back at her. "Darcy, honey, have you considered the possibility that the reason God did this to you is because Trevor is refusing to join this church and have a relationship with the only one true God?"

Darcy quickly lifted her head from staring at the table and glared at Preacher Dave. "What!" She stood from her chair. "What are you saying?"

"Darcy, honey," another elder said. "Sometimes we just don't understand that when there's sin in the camp, so to speak, terrible things can happen."

"I can't believe what I'm hearing," Darcy said.

"Come on, Darcy. You have to consider why this happened," Dave said. "Please. Sit back down."

"Don't tell me to sit down," she shouted. "Do you really expect me to believe that God took my child because my husband doesn't go to church?"

"Darcy," Dave said, failing in his attempt to interrupt.

"Even I have a bigger opinion of God than that. This is unbelievable. I give up. There's no sense in arguing with you guys." She grabbed her purse and stormed out of the room and down the hallway toward the office. She pulled the office door open slightly and stuck her head through it. "Rhonda, take care of yourself, hon. I'll not be darkening the doors of this place ever again."

Rhonda's face blushed red and her mouth hung open, but she said nothing. Darcy continued her walk out of the building and into the parking lot. As soon as she got in her car and closed the door, she started crying—crying hard. She didn't move the car for almost fifteen minutes.

"How dare they!" she shouted, slamming both of her hands against the rim of the steering wheel. "How could they!"

CHAPTER 8

Empathy

"I think we all have empathy.
We may not have enough courage to display it."
~ Maya Angelou

Trevor, Darcy, and Dawn arrived at The Kentucky Horse Park Campground where the bluegrass festival was being held. They hadn't been there in a couple of years, so they were anxious to see their friends. They hadn't had the motorhome parked and set up for very long, when Judy rounded the corner into the campsite. "There they are," she said.

"Well, hey there," Darcy said. She walked to Judy for a hug. "I am so happy to see you."

"Hi, Aunt Judy," Dawn said.

"Good Lord. You're a grown woman. How have you been, sweetie?"

"I'm doing good. Finally graduated from high school."

"Wow, that's wonderful," Judy said, reaching for Dawn to hug her, too. "I just can't believe my little baby girl is all grown up."

"Oh, don't I know it," Darcy said. "I'm getting old."

"Where's the rest of those yayhoos?" Judy asked, looking around.

"Trevor took off with Ben and Kevin to see Woody. I need to get over there to see him too, here pretty quick."

"Mom, I'm going to go in and do some reading," Dawn said.

"Well, okay, honey."

After Dawn got inside and closed the door, Darcy looked at Judy and shook her head.

"She's still down after all this time?" Judy asked.

"You don't know the half of it. I'm surprised she graduated. She's turned into a regular little hellion, always out with her worthless friends. I just don't get it."

"Maybe I can get her aside and talk to her sometime this weekend—try to figure out what's going on with her. Is the church helping any?"

"Nope. No church. We haven't been back there since just after Tracy died."

"Really?"

"I've had a few friends from there call and visit from time to time, but I've about decided that our church is as backward as Trevor always made them out to be." Darcy grimaced and lowered her head, rubbing her temples.

"You okay?" Judy asked.

"Ah, this darn headache. I've been having them a lot over the past year. Doctors can't find anything wrong and they just tell me to take over-the-counter stuff. Doesn't help much."

"Hey, girl," Trevor shouted as he and Ben walked into camp.

"Hey, sweetie. How you doin'?" Judy said. Darcy turned her head away.

"Let's pick," Ben said. "We left Kevin over there with Woody. Preacher Stan and Doc are over there too, so who knows how long he'll be."

"You know what, you guys go ahead," Darcy said. "I'm going to go lie down. My head is killing me."

Darcy went inside, closing the door behind her. Trevor sighed and rubbed the back of his neck. He looked out across the field with sad eyes.

"Whoa. Are you guys okay?" Judy asked.

"I don't know, Judy. I really don't."

"I'm going to go check on Kevin," Ben said, sensing the tension.

Judy smiled at him and nodded, then turned her attention back to Trevor. "What in the heck's going on?" she said.

Trevor sighed again. "Judy, she hasn't touched her fiddle since Tracy passed away. It's been almost three years."

"But she told me before you guys got here that she had a headache."

"She's had that headache for about as long."

"Well, why would she even come here if she wasn't interested in the music anymore and didn't feel well?"

Trevor met Judy's eyes. "That's just it. She doesn't want to be here. Dawn doesn't want to be here either. I feel like I'm holding this family together by a thread." He turned his gaze back out into the field.

"Oh, Trevor. I am so sorry," Judy said.

"I just don't know what to do."

"Did she even bring her fiddle?" Judy asked.

"Oh, it's in there. But only because I packed it myself."

They both fell silent for several minutes as they gazed into the field together. Then Trevor said, "You know, I think I'm going to walk back over there and see what those guys are doing. You want to come with me?"

"Sure. It'll be good to see them."

With Trevor and the others gone, the campsite was quiet. Inside, Dawn was in the back bedroom reading while Darcy slept on the couch. Darcy awoke when she heard Dawn rustling in the refrigerator. She saw that Dawn had put her shoes on and her hair was freshly brushed.

"What are you looking for, honey?"

"Nothing, Mom. I'm just getting a bottle of water. Go back to sleep." Dawn opened the door to leave.

"Where are you going?"

"I'm just going to take a walk, Mom. Please, just go back to sleep."

Dawn shook her head and closed the door. Darcy was alone. She rolled over on her back, rested her arm on her forehead, and stared at the light fixture in the ceiling. She went back to sleep and napped for another thirty minutes before getting up, brushing her hair, then going back out to sit in a lawn chair. She crossed her feet and propped them up on the seat of the picnic table. She put her glass of tea in the chair's cup holder. Her sunglasses reflected the sun underneath the brim of her old gardening hat. She threw her long blonde hair over the chair and rested her head back.

The campsite stayed perfectly still long enough for Darcy to finish about half of her tea and watch three deer slowly graze across the field beyond the fence. Judy quietly walked into the camp-site and sat on the picnic table next to Darcy's feet. She didn't say anything, her long shiny red hair ablaze in the afternoon sun. She stared at Darcy from behind her sunglasses.

"I like that hat," she said, finally breaking the silence.

"You've seen this hat a thousand times," Darcy said.

"I know. But I still like it."

"Thanks."

"You okay?" Judy asked.

"I think you should only get to ask me that once a day," Darcy said.

"Maybe. You know I love ya girl, and I worry about ya."

"I worry about me too, sometimes."

A voice chimed from the road that encircled the park. "Hey there. Haven't seen you in a while."

Darcy and Judy both turned, looking over the tops of their sunglasses. It was Jack Hanford.

"I didn't know if we were ever going to see you around here again," he said.

"And yet, here I am," Darcy said, with a stern look in her eyes.

"I guess I'll see you around."

"I guess."

"Darcy. What is it with you two?" Judy asked, as Jack walked away.

"I don't even know, anymore. Maybe I just have a problem with arrogant asses."

"Well, he has asked about you for the past two years, wondering where you guys were. I don't get it."

Darcy took a sip of her tea. "You want a glass?"

"No, I'm good. What's your issue with Jack?"

Once again, Darcy stared into the field, wondering where the deer went. Then she lowered her gaze into her glass of tea.

"What is it, Darcy?"

Darcy took in a deep breath. "Do you remember way back when we first came across Jack and his band, like fifteen years ago?"

Judy thought for a minute. "Yeah, I guess I do."

"Ben had gone over to jam with them that morning he met Jack."

"Oh, I do remember you guys talking about it. Yes."

"Well, I've never told this to anyone before, but shortly after Ben went over there, I followed him, thinking I was going to listen to them play. But just as I got there, I heard Ben and Jack talking and I froze just around the corner of their camper, out of sight. I overheard Jack telling Ben that a classically trained violin player had no place trying to play this music."

"What?"

"Yep. I was so shaken. He may as well have ripped my heart from me and stomped it on the ground."

"Honey, you have to take that crap with a grain of salt. I can't believe you've been carrying that around with you all these years."

"I know, but I was so embarrassed for eavesdropping. I ran away as soon as I heard it, and came back here to the camp."

"Dang, girl. You don't have to prove anything to anybody. You can play circles around all these fiddlers."

"I don't know, Judy. I doubt that I could do much of anything now. I was so proud of Tracy and enjoyed watching her so much that my own playing just didn't seem important anymore. Now, none of it seems important."

"Sweetie, you had a dream, and you tried to give your dream to Tracy. You can't do that. Yes, Tracy was a beautiful and talented young lady. But honey, she was living her own dream, not yours."

Darcy took off her sunglasses and hung them from the top of her shirt. She looked up from her tea and looked at Judy with her red swollen eyes. "I don't know what you mean. What has that got to do with Jack?"

"Honey, forget Jack. You're letting Jack and people like him steal your soul. Because of people like that, you tossed your dream to Tracy like someone would lateral pass a football."

Darcy chuckled. "Well, I don't know about that."

"Look, Tracy lived her dream. Oh, how she lived her dream. But you didn't give her that dream. You were God's gift to her to help her live out the dream He gave her."

"I don't understand."

Judy took off her sunglasses too, and laid them on the picnic table. She thought a minute and then turned back and looked at Darcy. "Here's what I think. I know you've heard it from Preacher Stan, but I think God plants a dream in each of us before we're even born. Then he entrusts us with the gifts we need to pursue that dream. I think most kids know it, though they would never be able to understand it. I'm pretty sure that's what Jesus was trying to tell us when He said we would do well to be like the little children. All too often, we grow away from the dream God gave us in order to do what is right in the eyes of society, often being told that what we love is impractical—that we should do what is responsible."

Judy leaned forward and put her hands on Darcy's knees. "Honey, your dream is yours. God gave it to you. You didn't give it to Tracy. You buried it."

Darcy covered her eyes behind one hand, still holding her iced tea in the other. "I just feel so angry," she said. "I'm angry with Jack. My marriage is in chaos. My daughter hates me. I've lost faith in my church. I'm even angry at God. Why should I trust anything He gives me? He took my little girl away."

She placed her glass back in the holder, lowered her face into both hands, and sobbed. Judy stood and put her arms around Darcy, stroking her hair. "It's okay to be mad at God," Judy said. "He can take it. But there's a secret to healing from the pain others have caused you."

"A secret?"

"Well, it really isn't a secret, I guess. But empathy is where you need to start. Do you know what empathy is?"

"Of course I know what empathy is," Darcy said, wiping her eyes with the sleeve of her shirt. "But what does that have to do with me?"

Judy sat back up on the picnic table. "Honey, I'm convinced that when people hurt us, it's because they don't understand us. When we hurt others, or are angry with them, it's because we don't understand them."

"Yeah, maybe," Darcy said, listening more intently.

"Take a look at the anger you're experiencing right now. You don't know anything about Jack. All you really know is that you don't think he likes you and that he's arrogant. What you haven't considered is why he is the way he is. You don't know what he has been through that made him that way."

"I know," Darcy said. "But he's just so infuriating."

"I don't know what the disagreements between you and Trevor are, but you know, he lost a daughter too—just like you. He had no more experience than you, trying to cope with the enormity of that. He's trying to process all that while trying to help you process it. That's my guess, anyway."

Darcy turned her gaze from Judy back out into the field. "I know."

"And poor Dawn, Judy continued. "She lost her big sister and probably the only hero she has ever known. And you haven't lost faith in your church, sweetie. You've lost faith in the men who lead it. They are the ones who hurt you—not the church. While they might not want to accept it, they are fallible men, carrying a couple hundred years of conservative church evolution on their shoulders."

"When did you get so smart?"

"Hey, I know stuff," Judy giggled.

They both laughed, giving the air a chance to thin out. Darcy quietly allowed Judy's wisdom to sink in. But then her smile turned to sadness once again. "Why are you telling me all this?"

"All I'm saying, Darcy, is that when you get crossways with the world, you need to at least try to understand where the world is coming from. Those people have had experiences and hurts too. You know, walk a mile in their moccasins."

"What does that even mean?"

"I guess that just popped into my head because I read that poem a few days ago."

"What poem?"

"It's called *Judge Softly*, by Mary Lathrap, from the late 1800s, I think. All I remember is that it ends with, 'Take the time to walk a mile in his moccasins.' I've heard that for years, but when I actually saw it in context, it made so much more sense to me. I just think we need to be really careful when we start criticizing others."

"So, why would God take my baby from me?"

Judy leaned back with her elbows on the picnic table and lowered her head back, staring at the darkening sky.

"That one, my dear, is a tough one. I can't presume to know why God does what he does. But he sure has one sweet little angel in heaven with that one. All I can figure is that the only way we can understand utter joy is by feeling utter sadness and pain."

"God, I miss her so much," Darcy said.

"I know you do, sweetie. I know you do. We all do. But this has left a really big hole in your heart, and it grieves everyone to see you go through this."

"So all this anger is my fault?"

"Of course not. You're feeling what any mother would feel. But when people cross you, you can't just cut them off. Take a quick second to imagine what they may have been through to bring them to that point in their life with that specific attitude. There are reasons that even they may not be aware of."

"So their history becomes my problem then?"

"No, no, no. You can't fix it. Just know it. If you empathize with them, you are the beneficiary. If their attack isn't met with defensiveness, perhaps that little wall will begin to crumble."

"Maybe," Darcy said. "I just don't think there is anything I could have said to sway the minds of Dave and those elders. Tracy died because Trevor wouldn't go to that church? Are you kidding me?"

"Calm down, sweetie. You're doing it again."

Darcy glared at Judy before putting her sunglasses back on. "Have I ever told you how much I dislike people telling me to calm down?"

"You're as Irish as I am," Judy said. "I know it makes you want to spit nails. But that doesn't change the fact that you need to have some empathy for the people around you."

"So you think God wanted me to be a fiddler before I was even born?"

"Well, I think he wanted you to touch the hearts of people with your music, so he entrusted you with the gifts you needed to pursue that. You had a choice as you grew older whether or not to use those gifts and whether or not to ignore your dream. God always gives us those choices. Everything is a choice. The only thing I can think of that we don't get to choose is whether or not to make a choice, even if we choose to do nothing. You know, kinda like you right now."

Darcy laughed. "Well, that was harsh."

"I know, honey, but I'll be honest. The people who know you and love you are dying a little inside when you don't play. They know your heart, and they know that aside from your husband and your girls, your heart is in that fiddle. And what's even worse, I see you dying inside too because you have your heart locked up in that case in there."

"Yeah, I don't even know why Trevor packed it. I told him I wouldn't be playing it."

"Well dang, sweetie. Don't you think it's eating him up too, knowing that your fiddle is every bit as much a part of you as your arm? You have to know that he packed it hoping against all hope that you might play it."

Darcy thought for several minutes, digesting all that Judy had said. "I just don't know what to do."

They heard footsteps, and looked up together to see Doc walking in. "Hey, ladies. Hope I'm not interrupting anything."

"Hey, Doc, not at all. Come on in," Darcy said, glancing at Judy and silently imploring her to end their conversation.

"You don't have to do anything right now," Judy told Darcy quietly. Then she stood up for a hug. "How are you doing Doc?"

"Doin' good, doin' good," he said. After he hugged Judy, he leaned over and kissed Darcy on the cheek.

"How are you doing, sweetie?" he asked.

"Oh, I'm fine. Judy was just sitting here trying to get all wise on me."

"Anything I can help with? I've been told numerous times that I'm a wise guy."

"I don't reckon. Hey, didn't you do some research awhile back about people leaving the church?" Darcy asked.

"I did. It was the *Dechurched Project*. We called the book that came out of it, *Church Refugees*. Why? Do you know someone leaving the church?"

"Well, I did."

"You left the church? Dang! You want to talk about it?"

"Not really," Darcy said, smiling at Judy. "Not now, anyway. I'm about talked out."

"I can take a hint," Judy said. "Hey Doc, do you have a few minutes to come over to our camp? Tom was asking about you."

"Sure. I haven't seen him yet this trip."

Judy turned her head away so Doc couldn't see and stuck her tongue out at Darcy. They both smiled as Judy and Doc walked out of the camp. Darcy's smile faded as she turned her gaze across the field, once again thinking about her anger and how she wanted her life to be like it used to be.

It was an unusually quiet afternoon at the festival. Darcy thought maybe it just wasn't going to be as crowded that year as it usually was. But she was relaxing in the silence, enjoying the sun on her face and the gentle breeze.

"Oh God, what to do, what to do," she said with a deep sigh.

She shook her glass, rattling the ice, and realized it was empty. She climbed into the motorhome for a refill and to straighten things up a little around the kitchen. She looked over and noticed her fiddle case in the overhead bunk above the driver's seat. "I still don't know why he had to bring that thing," she said under her breath, shaking her head.

She filled her glass, and looked over at the fiddle again. Her knees weakened as she put the pitcher back in the refrigerator. She took her glass to the dining table and sat down, again looking at her fiddle. But this time she stared at it for what seemed to be an eternity as the memories of playing it flooded her thoughts. Tears filled her eyes as she remembered the times she watched Tracy on stage and the audience whistling and cheering. Darcy smiled through her tears and dropped her head.

"Oh, Tracy," she said. Darcy wiped her eyes and lifted her head to stare at the case once again. "Okay, let's see." She stood and got the case down from the overhead. She put it on the table and opened it, smiling like she was looking at a newborn baby. She gently rubbed the strings with the tips of her fingers. "Oh, how I've missed you," she said. She closed her eyes, leaned her head back, and looked at the ceiling. "Is this it, God?"

After a few agonizing minutes of debate, she finally took her fiddle out of the case and began to pluck each string, turning the pegs in the peghead to tune it up. She still didn't need a tuner or a pitch fork to get things just right, fine tuning each string relative to the other. She placed it aside and took the bow from the hooks in the lid and tightened the fine horsehair. It shimmered in the sunlight streaming through the picture window over the dining table. She took the rosin from the pocket in the case and slid it up and down the length of the horsehair.

"Am I really going to do this?" she thought.

She picked up the fiddle again and tucked it under her chin, cupping the neck gently in her left hand. She ran the bow across each string, first one at a time to fine tune them, and then droned one string against the next to make sure the intonation was just right. First the E with the A, then the A with the D, and finally the D with the G. "Perfect."

Finally, Darcy slowly began to play an old ballad piece that she had learned back in her days at the Boston Conservatory—simple, but beautiful. She played as though she had never stopped at all. Each note was flawless. But then tears filled her eyes again and she stopped playing. She turned and leaned against the dining table and dropped her head. "God, please. If Judy is right and my music really does touch people, please help me out here."

She wiped her eyes with the back of her bowing hand and put the fiddle back under her chin. She heard the sound of Trevor's guitar in her head and began playing an old ballad called Maiden's Prayer. Darcy closed her eyes and let the music take her back to a happy time. She let herself go into a trance with the music surrounding her.

Trevor was walking back to camp, alone, when he rounded the back of the motorhome and heard the fiddle. He tried to figure out where the music was coming from because he didn't think it would be Darcy, yet he knew it was. He stopped and listened. "My God," he whispered.

He quietly walked up to the door, dropping his head so as not to be seen from inside. He sat motionless on the steps and listened. The sound of Darcy's fiddle gave him goose bumps. He crossed his arms on his knees and lowered his forehead to rest on them.

Darcy played one tune after another, eventually taking on some of the faster pieces that she and Tracy used to play with twin fiddles. Trevor was crying and smiling and laughing to himself, then crying again.

After several minutes, Trevor heard footsteps coming around the motorhome. He looked up and saw Dawn freeze as she heard the fiddle. Her mouth dropped open as she stared at Trevor, when she realized what was happening. Tears came to her eyes as well. She smiled and made the motion of clapping her hands without actually clapping them. Her huge smile warmed Trevor's heart as she ducked her head and eased over to stand next to him.

She rubbed his back and then put her arm around his shoulders as they listened...and cried.

CHAPTER 9

Attitude

*"Nothing can stop the man with the right mental attitude
from achieving his goal; nothing on earth can help the man
with the wrong mental attitude."*
~ Thomas Jefferson

The following year, Trevor and Darcy waited until Saturday to go to the festival in Lexington. They arrived at mid-morning and set up camp as usual—but this time, without Dawn. After everything was set up, Trevor brought his old clawhammer banjo and Darcy's fiddle case out of the motorhome. "I'm in no hurry to walk around," Trevor said. "You wanna play some?"

"Sure," Darcy said. She took her case from him, removed the fiddle and bow, and started tuning. Judy showed up on cue, throwing her arms in the air as she entered the campsite.

"Hello, my children," she said.

"Well, aren't we chipper today?" Darcy laughed.

Judy hugged them both, and sat on top of the picnic table. "We missed you last night," she said.

"Sorry about that," Trevor said. "We had a bit of drama at the house last night. Dawn decided she didn't want to come anymore. She thinks she's too old to be hanging around with her parents." Darcy shook her head and smiled.

"And what do you think about that, little missy?" Judy asked, noticing Darcy's reaction.

"Well, I was hurt last night. But now, after thinking about it a while, it seems pretty funny." Trevor and Judy both opened their mouths in shock.

"What in the world are you talking about?" Trevor asked.

"Oh, I was just thinking back to the way I was with my folks. The grief I caused them. They had this idea that I was going to go up and join the Cincinnati Symphony Orchestra when I graduated from the Conservatory. I had no intention of doing that, and it killed them. I was such a pill, I actually gloated in the defiance. This is just my due."

Judy shook her head and looked at Trevor in disbelief. "Anyway, I'm glad you guys are here," Judy said. "Jimmy is asking if we can fill a spot this afternoon. Apparently, one of the bands is going to be late. I don't know who it is, but he's in a bind. What do you guys think?"

Darcy nodded, and Trevor smiled. "We can do that," he said. "Where are those other two yayhoos?"

"Lord, I don't know," Judy said. "Probably over there eating. I was gonna go walk around anyway. I'll track them down. I'll see you two in a bit."

As Judy walked away, Darcy continued to tune her fiddle. "Let's mess around with *Solder's Joy*," she said.

Trevor started frailing his banjo, and Darcy joined in. They played on it for several minutes just warming up. While Darcy had played quite a bit over the past year, she wanted to do more of these old parking lot tunes. After a few minutes, she looked up and saw Jack Hanford standing in front of the motorhome, staring at them.

"Let me guess. You finally gave up bluegrass and are turning old-time now."

"Shut up and keep walking, Jack," she said.

"All right. All right. I'm going," he said as he turned and walked away.

"What an ass," she said, smiling at Trevor.

Trevor shook his head. "You two need to kiss and make up."

"He still irritates me," Darcy said.

They continued to play one old-time tune after another for almost thirty minutes, when Judy returned with Ben and Kevin.

"Heeeyyyyy," Kevin screamed as soon as they got near the camp. Trevor and Darcy could hear them long before they saw them.

"Good grief," Darcy said.

Trevor laughed. "They're here."

When they finally arrived in the camp, there were greetings and hugs all around. Then Kevin jumped up on the picnic table while Ben headed straight for the door. "Anything to drink?" Ben shouted.

"In the fridge," Darcy said, shaking her head. "Help yourself."

"Okay, we need to throw together a set list," Judy said. "What's it going to be?"

"Well, we need to keep it bluegrass," Trevor said, looking at Darcy.

"What? I know. I know," she said with a grin.

Ben came out with several bottles of water in his arms and passed them around before he sat on a lawn chair. Trevor and Darcy laid their instruments back in the cases and started brainstorming the songs they would do during their set later that day. Darcy thought about how much it seemed like old times.

"Ladies and gentlemen, Fiddler's Roost," the emcee shouted as the five of them paraded onto the stage and the audience cheered. After a few seconds of fine-tuning, Judy pressed into her mandolin and kicked off a song called *Daniel Prayed*. Darcy sang out like the powerhouse she always was. "I read about a man one day, who wasted not his time away. He prayed to God, every mornin', noon, and night."

Trevor and Judy gathered around the single microphone with her and sang some of the tightest harmony the folks there had ever heard. Woody was standing next to Jerry at the sound board. "Dang," he said, in amazement.

"Yeah, dang," Jerry said.

Ben watched the three singing as he played rhythm guitar with his signature heavy hand. Kevin watched them all from behind and kept impeccable time for the group on his bass. They were all smiling and having the time of their lives. The crowd was clearly having a good time as well. Their eyes were glued to the stage.

Stan and Doc were walking by when they heard the emcee announce the group, so they had stopped and turned to watch from the edge of the rows of chairs.

"I am so glad to see that little girl get out of her funk," Stan said.

"Yeah, really," Doc said. "I need to stop by and talk to her in a bit—see how she's getting along."

Darcy and the band played their 45-minute set, and ended with a fiddle tune to a standing ovation. They took a bow and went on their way, laughing and comparing notes as the sun began to set.

"That was amazing," Darcy said.

"I'm starving," Kevin said. "You guys wanna go get something to eat?"

"I'm going to go back to camp and check on Tom," Judy said.

"Yeah, I'm just going to go back to camp as well," Darcy said. "You guys go ahead. I'm beat." Darcy reached for Trevor's banjo case. "I'll take that back, hon."

"Thanks," he said. "I won't be long."

Darcy walked off alone toward the motorhome, her fiddle strapped over one shoulder, while she carried Trevor's banjo case in the other hand. It was getting dark when she ran into Stan and Doc. "Hey, Doc. Hey, Preacher Stan," she said. "How are you guys doing? Good to see ya."

"Let me take that. It must weigh a ton," Doc said as he took the banjo case from Darcy.

"That it does," she said. "Thanks."

"That was a powerful performance, sweetie," Stan said. Doc nodded in agreement.

"Oh, you guys saw that? It did feel really good."

After they walked a little farther, Stan said, "Hey, you guys go on ahead. I'm gonna go see what Woody's up to."

"Okay," Doc said. "I'll catch up in a bit."

"I'll see you later," Darcy said.

"He's such a good guy," she said to Doc after Stan had left.

"Yep, he's a good friend. I think he's a little worried about you, though."

"Worried? How so?" she asked.

"Well, are you guys going to church anywhere?"

"Oh, that. No. I'm not sure I ever will. I haven't lost faith in God, but I've pretty much lost faith completely in the men that lead the churches."

"You certainly aren't alone," Doc said. "I really don't think these church leaders understand just how much they push people away while trying to reach their level of perfection."

"Just set it down there by the door, Doc. You want something to drink or eat?"

"I'll take a glass of tea if you have it," Doc said.

"Sure enough. Make yourself at home." Darcy climbed inside with her fiddle still on her shoulder. She laid it up in the overhead bunk where it normally rested. "So are you working on anything interesting these days, Doc?" Darcy asked through the window as she got the pitcher from the refrigerator. She poured the tea over some ice.

"Not really," he said as he sat in a lawn chair. "I've actually been staying pretty busy with that last project I did."

Darcy kicked the door open and walked down the steps with the two glasses of tea, then slammed the screen door shut with her elbow. "Here you go," she said, handing him a glass and sitting in the chair next to him. "Whew," she exhaled a deep satisfied breath. "My feet are killing me."

"You guys did really good up there tonight."

"Well, thanks, Doc. I appreciate that." They both took a sip of their tea and looked around to see who was walking where.

Resuming their previous conversation, Doc said, "So, you don't think you'll be returning to the church, then?"

"No, Doc. I don't think so. I'm done."

He looked at her and smiled.

"What?" she asked.

"Oh, nothing. It was just ironic that you used that word, *done*. In my last research project, we had identified a group of Christians that we called, *The Dones*. It was about the folks that never let go of their faith in God but were done with organized religion for various reasons."

"And what reasons might those be?"

"Well, you know. They were hurt by somebody in the church or it was just too hard to pursue their ministry under the control of church leadership. So they decided they would continue to follow Christ but pursue their ministries on their own terms."

"So, I guess I'm a *Done* then," Darcy said, smiling at Doc.

"I guess you are." He took another sip of his tea.

"Well, it just pisses me off, Doc. All this talk about the Great Commission, and how we need to be bringing people to the Lord and all that, while church leaders are running people off."

"True, but it certainly isn't all church leaders. Far from it. But the perception of that judgment sure is out there. There are those who feel like it's their responsibility to guard our souls for us—to intervene in our personal relationship with God. When that happens, they almost always end up causing more harm than good.

But on the other hand, the pain they cause is really only a perceived problem."

"What do you mean?" Darcy asked.

"Well, when people throw something at you, attack you, or judge you, or whatever—it can only hurt you as much as you let it."

"Say what?" Darcy squinted her right eye, smirking.

"It's true. What people do or say to you is only served by your reaction to it. What I've learned through the years is that attitude is everything when it comes to making choices and reacting."

"So, you're saying I have a bad attitude then?" Darcy stared at Doc, trying but failing to look angry or offended. He looked back at her, tickled by her crooked face, and they both started laughing.

"Well, if the shoe fits," he said.

"I guess I get it," Darcy said. "So if people are really rude to me, I can get all up in their face or I can smile and walk away. My response is completely up to me and nobody else."

"Exactly."

"Wow. When you think about it, that could apply to almost anything."

"I have thought about it, and yes it could," he said.

"Shut up," Darcy laughed, shaking her head.

"But really, Darcy, when those guys tried to make you believe that Tracy died because there was sin in the camp, your reaction was completely up to you—a choice only you could make. Your attitude toward the conversation led you to get angry and storm out, right?"

"You got that right."

"You could have chosen to react differently. Choices are always about attitude. When they judged you like that, you could have chosen to believe that they didn't know the Bible like you did. You could have chosen not to be drawn in by their ignorance of the nature of Jesus Christ. You could have chosen to stand, smile, and quietly walk out the door. You make those choices based on attitude. You don't have to leave a church angry, slamming doors, trying to make your point. You can leave a church quietly because you disagree with the principles of their teaching."

"I suppose."

"Look, sweetie, those men aren't evil. Misinformed, maybe, but they love God and are as well-intentioned as we are. They wanted to help you. Deciding not to go back there is fine, but judging those guys for their mistakes puts you in the same cage. Attitude is the difference. The attitude you choose could lead to forgiveness, which is more about you than it is about them. When you carry the attitude of forgiveness, it frees your soul to live life to its fullest. You can't let those guys take that away from you, when they aren't even around you anymore."

"I get it. I get it. So I really need to spend some time thinking about my attitude and learn how to think before I react."

"Right. Well, unless you're about to rear end a car, then you probably shouldn't think too much."

Darcy reached over and slapped his arm. "Shut up." Again, they laughed and sipped their tea. "So what else have you learned about these folks you call *The Dones*? She asked. "Do you think they're going to be okay without organized religion? I guess I should say WE. Are WE going to be okay without organized religion?"

"Well, the thing about doing church in a church building is that it's a convenient place to gather with other Christians, hear God's word, worship, sing, witness baptisms, and all those things you love doing on Sunday morning. But that's just it. It's a convenience—not a necessity. There is nothing special about the building. But the one magical thing that happens there is community. Being around friends and family and serving each other is really important to being a Christian. In fact, serving each other may be one of the most important things there is. So when you make a decision to leave organized religion, you need to first understand and be clear about your community. If you're leaving in order to better serve your ministry, then that may be where your community lies. I think that's perfectly fine. But if you leave organized religion and allow yourself to become an island, Satan has you right where he wants you. You lose your strength and he builds on your negative attitude."

"I sure hadn't thought about all that," Darcy said. "I guess I did kind of set myself up on an island as far as my faith goes. Trevor certainly never gave me any encouragement to go to church. Never has. And these days, Dawn is just mad at the world, so she's little help."

"I know. That must have been a terrible thing for her to have to go through."

"It's been really hard the last few years," Darcy said. "She is so angry. Trevor and I are fighting all the time about how to handle her. She defies anything we have to say. I think we should give her space to grow through it, but all he can think about is getting her to buckle down and find the right college."

"Hey there, y'all," Trevor said, entering the campsite.

"Hey, Trev," Doc said. "Did you leave everyone well over there?"

Darcy turned her head away and rested it in her hand, covering her eyes.

"They're all doing fine," Trevor said. "Just yacking it up about the best guitar wood."

Early the next morning, Darcy awoke to the sound of Trevor outside, folding chairs and rolling up the awning. It was a day for goodbyes and a few tears. It would be another year before many of the friends there would see each other again.

She listened peacefully for several minutes before she got out of bed and got dressed for the day. She took her fiddle out of the case and tightened up her bow. Even so early in the morning, her fiddle lifted a beautiful melody in the air that could be heard several campsites away.

Outside, Trevor smiled and went about his work.

Trevor and Darcy returned home later that afternoon to find Dawn lying in her bed, her clothes strewn all over her bedroom. "Come on, honey. Get out of bed and clean this mess up," Darcy said.

"Mom. Please," Dawn said, rolling over with her pillow covering her head. "I'll get up in a little while."

"Now, Dawn," Trevor yelled from the living room. He walked up into her room, and said," This is getting ridiculous, young lady. You need to pull yourself together and get started on those brochures. You need to start filling out some applications, for crying out loud."

"Fine," she said, sitting up and throwing her pillow across the room. "But you know what? I don't even know if I want to go to college."

She bolted out of the bed, out of her room, and into the bathroom, slamming the door behind her. Trevor looked at Darcy, rolled his eyes, and threw his hands in the air. "What is going on around here?"

Dawn didn't go to college. Instead, she met the boy of her dreams, Rick Tanner, and got married. Trevor and Darcy were disappointed in her decision, but liked Rick just fine. He was a residential building contractor, and was doing well for himself to be so young. Trevor thought Rick's motorcycle was really cool, so that was always the center of their conversation when they were together.

Darcy was relieved that the hole in Dawn's heart was finally being filled. Darcy often remembered what Doc had said about attitude. She played it over and over again in her mind. She was comforted on many occasions just knowing that she had control over her attitude and her reactions to life. It was much easier to simply turn things over to God. But she often still wondered about the things he said related to community and the importance of it. She didn't think she had done well there.

One Saturday afternoon, Dawn and Rick showed up at the house unannounced, walking in the back door to the sound of her mom and dad playing in the music room. Oh, how she loved the sound of them playing together and the joyful memories it conjured up. That day, it was particularly sweet to her ears.

"Mom," she yelled. The music stopped.

"In here, sweetie," Darcy said.

Dawn and Rick walked into the music room, holding hands. "You guys sound great," Rick said.

"Well, thanks, hon," Darcy said. "We're just working on some stuff for a contest that may or may not ever happen, someday, maybe."

"Oh Mom," Dawn said. "When are you going to do it?"

Trevor peered at Darcy with squinted eyes. "Yeah, Mom. When are you going to do it?"

"Lord, I don't know, you guys. Someday."

"Whenever it is, you're going to kick butt," Dawn said. Then a huge smile came over Dawn's face. "We have news," she said. Rick put his arm around her and she leaned into him. They both beamed.

Darcy jumped from her seat and lifted her fiddle and bow over her head. "Oh my God! Oh my God! Oh my God!" She stared at her little girl until finally, Dawn nodded.

"Yes."

"Oh my God!" Darcy put her fiddle and bow in the chair and lunged toward Dawn, throwing her arms around her. "You're going to have a baby! Oh my God!"

Trevor stood and put his guitar in its stand and reached to shake Rick's hand. "Congratulations, son. That's awesome."

Darcy let Dawn go, and turned to hug Rick. Dawn fell into her daddy's arms. She hadn't been this happy in years. After several minutes of celebration, Darcy and Trevor stepped back, and everyone sat down. "This is so exciting," Darcy said. "I am so tickled for you guys."

"It is pretty amazing," Dawn said.

Rick was still in a state of shock over the whole thing, but was obviously happy.

"There is one thing I'd like to ask," Dawn said.

"Sure, honey, what is it?" Trevor asked.

"Well, we've talked it over, and I'm kinda hoping for a girl. But either way, is it okay with you guys if we name the baby Tracy?"

"Aw!" Tears welled up in Darcy's eyes. "Of course it's okay with us, sweetie. That's the most beautiful thing I've ever heard."

Dawn got up from the couch and wrapped both arms around her mom. They sat crying together for a few minutes before Darcy shook her off. "Okay, okay. That's enough of that. This is a happy day. Lemonade all around," she said as she jumped to her feet and led the parade to the kitchen.

After an afternoon of celebration, Rick and Dawn climbed on his motorcycle and thundered off down the street.

"I love those guys," Trevor said, his eyes glued to that beautiful motorcycle.

Darcy slapped his arm. "Shut up."

Trevor and Darcy skipped the bluegrass festival that year. It was nearing Dawn's due date, and Darcy wanted to be close by and available. Dawn not only gave birth to the girl she had hoped for, but she gave birth to twins. God had doubled down on her prayer.

Trevor and Darcy were the grandparents of two baby girls, the joy of the family. The twins, Tracy Lynn and Alison, even went to the bluegrass festival with Papaw and Nana on occasion, to give Rick and Dawn a nice break. The twins grew to love Darcy's fiddle playing. They would sit on the floor and listen to every note, way beyond a toddler's normal attention span. When they were old enough to hold the bow, Darcy brought the little quarter-sized fiddle out of the closet that she had used to teach Tracy.

One day, when the twins were four years old, Rick and Dawn came to the house to pick them up. Trevor and Darcy had just returned from the festival with them. "Before you go," Darcy said, "come back here and listen to this."

Everyone retired to the music room. Darcy took the tiny fiddle out of its case and handed it to Tracy Lynn. "Play that new tune Nana taught you," Darcy said.

With every bit of concentration a four-year-old could muster, Tracy Lynn started playing *Mary Had a Little Lamb*. The squeaks and scratches only briefly interrupted the melody. Dawn dropped her jaw and covered her mouth. "Oh my God, how cute," she said, tears pooling in her eyes.

Then she covered her heart with both hands and looked at the picture of her and Tracy hanging on the wall, when they were the twins' age. When Tracy Lynn was finished playing, everyone applauded, including little Alison. You could tell she was so proud of her sister. Dawn sat down and hugged Tracy Lynn as Darcy took the fiddle from her.

"What a great job you did, Tracy Lynn," Dawn said. Then she glanced at Alison. "You too, Ali. You did a great job supporting your sister. Such a good girl, you are."

"You can just let them stay here tonight if you want, honey," Darcy said.

"That would be great, Mom. We're on the bike anyway, and were headed to some friends' house. We were planning to come back later and get them in the car, but if you're okay with them staying here tonight, that would be perfect."

"No problem at all," Darcy said. "You girls want to stay with Nana and Papaw tonight?"

"Yeah," they shouted.

As Rick and Dawn walked out of the back door, Trevor noticed it was drizzling rain. "You guys be careful out there. The roads will be slick."

"Yeah, will do, Mr. M," Rick said. They climbed on and headed down the road. Thirty minutes later, when Darcy was in the music room with the twins and Trevor was reading the paper at the dining room table, the phone rang. It was Rick.

Trevor and Darcy ran down the hospital hallway with Tracy Lynn and Alison. Trevor then held the girls back while Darcy ran faster when she saw Rick, sitting in a chair, hunched over with his face in his hands. Dawn had lost her grip on Rick's waist when he swerved to avoid an accident. He hit a curb, and she fell off the back of the motorcycle.

When Darcy touched Rick's shoulder, he looked up with red swollen eyes. "Dawn is dead."

CHAPTER 10

Devotion

"True strength lies in submission which permits one to dedicate his life, through devotion, to something beyond himself."
~ Henry Miller

"It's impossible for us to know why God does what he does, especially at times like these. But we do know that God is love, and without such unimaginable pain, we would never know the joy made full that he promised us through our Lord, Jesus Christ."

Preacher Stan conducted Dawn's funeral services at Darcy's request. It was difficult for him because he had known Dawn her entire life. She was such a beautiful young woman, so full of energy, and she herself had endured such unimaginable pain as a child, when she lost her sister.

"Dawn has left us now. She adored her husband, Rick. Her two little girls, Tracy Lynn and Alison, were the light of her life. But she loved her sister, Tracy, too. They are finally together again. I can only imagine Tracy playing her heavenly fiddle with Dawn, her biggest fan, at her side. When those two were small children, growing up around so much music, I was always amazed at the love they had for each other. A love instilled by their mother, Darcy. There was never a hint of jealousy between them. Seeing Tracy and Dawn together again, is one of the most beautiful sights I could imagine.

"Dawn was raising her twins to be the same way—to be best friends, to be respectful and loving. Dawn will most certainly be missed here on earth, but what a party she and Tracy must be having in heaven."

Darcy sat in the front pew with Tracy Lynn to her right and Alison to her left. Then Trevor and Rick on either side of them. It was the same place she sat when they buried Tracy. She never wanted to return to that church, but she couldn't imagine not burying Dawn alongside Tracy. It only made sense that they would have the service there. Stan spoke to Preacher Dave, and he agreed to allow Stan to preside over the funeral.

"You are all invited to join the family for a short graveside service. If you would like to participate, please follow the pallbearers and file out of these side doors. You may greet the family out there afterward," Stan said. Everyone stood, except Darcy.

"Are you coming, Nana?" Alison said.

"Yes, sweetie. I'll be along."

Rick put his arms around the twins and ushered them toward the door. Stan stepped down from the pulpit and joined Trevor, Doc, Judy, Ben, Kevin, and Woody, who had all surrounded Darcy. They stood that way without saying a word until the church had emptied. Darcy never looked up at them.

"Are you ready, honey?" Trevor asked.

She finally looked up at him, her eyes piercing. She said nothing, but stood and walked toward the door. Her friends walked silently behind her. When Darcy and the group arrived at the gravesite, they sat under the canopy, out of the hot sun, with Rick and the girls. Darcy sat motionless, staring at the ground. She didn't hear a word of what Stan was saying and only barely acknowledged those who were leaving after the proceedings were over.

"Darcy, honey. Come on. Let's go home," Trevor said. "Rick and the girls are already in the parking lot." It was the first thing she heard since leaving the building. She stood and looked around and saw that everyone had left except the close friends who walked with her to the cemetery.

"Are you okay?" Trevor asked.

She looked up at him with the same piercing eyes as before. "What do you mean, am I okay? No, I'm not okay. My girls are gone. They're dead. You son of a bitch, you should have never let her get on that damn motorcycle," She said, poking her finger at Trevor's chest.

"Okay. Okay. I'm sorry," he said. "Let's get to the car." He tried to put his arm around her.

"Don't touch me," she shouted, pushing him away. She stormed out across the lawn, toward the parking lot.

Trevor looked at his wife sadly. The others were clearly stunned at her outburst but they kept walking. Doc put his arm around Trevor. "Sorry, man. Don't take that personally. You know she's hurting."

"Oh, I know just how she feels. I feel the same way. Dawn shouldn't have been on that motorcycle."

Darcy was almost to the parking lot so she couldn't hear the conversation. But Judy, who was walking in front of Doc and Trevor, heard them. She stopped and turned, pointing her finger at Trevor. "Don't do that," she said.

"Don't do what?" Trevor asked.

"Don't blame yourself for what happened to Dawn. She was a grown woman and she loved being on that bike with Rick. Yes, Darcy is hurting terribly, but so are you. Don't you let her make you believe this is somehow your fault. Don't you do it."

Trevor broke down and cried. Judy threw her arms around him, and the others encircled them, putting their hands on Trevor's shoulders.

"Come on, buddy," Stan said. "Let's get you home."

When they walked into the back door of Trevor and Darcy's house, it was an eerie replay of what had taken place when Tracy died. The group of friends tried to be a little upbeat, but it was a useless attempt.

"I can't," Darcy said, and she walked out of the kitchen into the music room. When she closed the door, everyone looked at Trevor.

"Is she going to be okay, man?" Ben asked.

"I don't know. She won't talk to me. She's really angry."

"Well, that's understandable," Doc said.

They all sat around the dining room table, chatting and munching on snacks. After about thirty minutes, they had started to forget about the pain and sadness a little and told fun stories, laughing about some of their memories.

They all fell silent when they heard the music room door open. Darcy darted through the kitchen and out the back door, not saying a word or looking at anyone. Trevor looked out the window and watched her walk across the backyard to the fence at the back of their property.

She stood at the fence, holding on to the top rail, one foot propped on the bottom rail. She stared into the woods, motionless. Trevor sat back down at the kitchen table. "She'll be fine," he said.

"Do you mind if I go talk to her?" Stan asked.

"Be my guest."

Doc slapped Stan's back as he got up from the table and headed toward the door. He walked slowly across the large green yard alongside the garage where the motorhome was parked. He looked around and saw the neighbor's cattle grazing and a few horses across the field. Yet with all that, Darcy was staring out into the woods behind the yard.

"Mind a little company?" Stan said as he came up behind her.

"Oh, I don't know if anyone needs to be around me right now, Stan," Darcy said with a whimper.

He stood next to her and noticed the tears on her cheeks and her puffy red eyes.

"I'm really sorry for being such a bitch," she said. "Excuse my French."

"Not to worry, we all have our days."

"Stan, I just don't know how I'm going to live."

"I don't know either, honey," he said.

Darcy stared at him, a puzzled look on her face. "What? Not exactly what I was expecting to hear."

"Oh. Well, you've been through a lot. I've seen a lot of things in all my years in ministry. I've watched people die under all kinds of circumstances. I've seen pain like you wouldn't believe, but living through the loss of two of your kids—that ranks way up there. I can't imagine the pain you're feeling."

"What I am, is pissed off. I'm so pissed off I could scream."

"Well, scream, then," Stan said.

"I think I was about to when you showed up."

"Oh. Sorry."

"That's okay. You're probably the one friend I needed to see right now, anyway. It's God I'm mad at. Well, him and Trevor. I just can't figure out what I've done to turn God against me. I'm just about convinced that this whole God thing is a huge mistake."

"I understand why you would feel that way," Stan said. "But right now, you probably need God more than you need me."

"Maybe. I keep thinking about what Dave told me after Tracy died. Do you really think God would be doing this because Trevor isn't a believer?"

"Of course not. Look, Dave and those guys are idiots."

Darcy's head spun to look at Stan, her eyes the size of silver dollars.

"Well, okay. Maybe not idiots," Stan said. "But they shouldn't be poisoning your mind with stuff like that. It is absolutely ridiculous to judge people in a way that is so contrary to the nature of Jesus Christ. Jesus never would have said or believed anything like that. Just know that all churches don't spew that stuff—even among the a cappella churches."

"I just don't get it, then. I could almost understand that better than anything else I have to work with."

"I know, honey. We'll never know why God does what He does. I guess it just isn't for us to know. What I do know is that without this kind of pain, we'll never understand the joy made full that Jesus prayed for."

"I just wish I knew how to get through this," Darcy said.

"Well, I can give you one word to ponder," Stan said. "Devotion."

"Devotion?"

"Devotion. You know. *Sticktoitiveness*."

"Okay?" she said.

"Life hands us all these challenges. God gives us the gift of choices. We get to choose what our response will be to any given set of circumstances."

"Yeah, I've been down this road."

"Well, through all of those distractions and decisions, what keeps us focused is devotion. Being devoted to God, devoted to your family, devoted to your dream—those points of devotion—that's what gets you through. God planted that seed of a dream so you can devote yourself to that, above all else. That is what gets you through life, even when the world keeps throwing obstacles in front of you."

"I get it, Stan. I really do. But I'm so empty right now. None of that really matters. Quite frankly, I don't even like Trevor. I don't feel like he understands a thing about me. It's a joke."

"Honey, you just need to heal. Life has knocked you down big time. No doubt about it. But you'll get back up. Your dreams will matter again. I promise."

"That's a pretty bold promise."

"Well, like I said, I've seen a lot of things. Recovery will come if you stay devoted and keep looking ahead."

"I suppose."

Stan turned around and leaned his back against the fence, putting his foot on the bottom rail. "Didn't you have a dream once to win some big fiddle contest?"

"Oh yeah. But that was years ago. It isn't going to happen. There are some talented kids out there winning that thing every year. Granny here doesn't stand a chance."

"Maybe, but that's a dream that could be your devotion—the bootstraps that you need to pull on."

"You can't be serious."

"Look, I know this day sucks, big time. But give yourself a few months and keep thinking about what you are devoted to."

"Well, those two grandbabies, for one thing. They're the only reason I have to breathe right now." Darcy lowered her head to the fence rail and started crying again.

Stan turned, and patted her back. "I know, honey. I know."

"Preacher Stan. The reason I got so angry with Trevor at the church is because Dawn wanted to get baptized."

Stan froze, then looked into the woods. "What? Why would that make you angry?"

"I wasn't angry at her for wanting to do it. I was so happy that she had grown so much and had accepted the Lord into her life. I was so mad that she was killed before she made it to the baptistery. Last week, I was really worried about what it meant. So, I went back to Dave to try to understand it all."

Stan rolled his eyes and turned his face away from her. "Oh, Lord."

"He told me that baptism was essential to salvation and that I probably wouldn't be seeing Dawn in heaven. So how can she be there with Tracy?" Darcy cried and fell to her knees, laying her forehead against the bottom rail. "Trevor should never have let her get on that motorcycle," she said, sobbing deeply, her face soaked in tears. "Rick shouldn't have either, but Trevor knew better."

Stan sat on the ground next to Darcy and wrapped his arms around her. But then, he was angry too. He gazed into the woods as he tried to console Darcy's broken heart. He was livid, knowing the legalism that led to Dave's comments. "Doesn't he know he's ripping this girl's heart out?" he thought.

He held on to his composure because he knew Darcy needed him. But what he wanted to do was go straight to the church and break Dave's legs. "What an idiot," he thought.

"Honey, it's okay. Dawn is fine. Dave doesn't get to make those judgments. He really doesn't. God knows that Dawn loves Jesus. I know baptism is important, but I just don't think God is so small that he would deny her His grace. In fact, I'm confident that He is a much bigger God than that."

"But how do you know?" she asked.

"Well," Stan said. "There's always Matthew 18, I think in verse 6. After telling us to be like little children and follow Him, Jesus says 'whoever causes one of these little ones who believe in me to stumble, it would be better for him to have a heavy millstone hung around his neck, and be drowned in the depths of the sea.' Now, I think that's pretty telling. He's talking about us. He's talking about you!"

Stan stayed quiet after that and let Darcy cry. He got comfortable on the ground. After several minutes, Darcy had gotten quiet. "Can I pray for you, honey?" Stan asked.

Darcy nodded and held tighter to his arm. He looked up at the sky that was beginning to darken. "Dearest heavenly Father, you are an awesome God. Today we've committed to you our sweet Dawn. She was so loved here on earth, Lord, and we know you will love her there with you. God, while we understand so little about our pain, we ask that you comfort those of us who remain here and heal this heart that has been broken. Please help Darcy to see through the pain and remain devoted to you. Help her to regain some clarity for her future, to gain strength, and to return to the path you set for her. Help her to see her dream again, Lord. Please help those among us who sit in judgement of your children, causing them to walk away from you in disgust. Help them to understand that it is you who owns the plan of salvation, not them. Please have mercy on their souls. It's in Jesus' holy name that we pray. Amen."

"Amen," Darcy whispered.

Stan stood and helped Darcy to her feet. She had become weak. She leaned on him heavily as they walked back toward the house.

Judy was looking out the kitchen window when she saw them coming, so when they had gotten near the steps, she opened the door for them. "Honey, do you want something to eat?" Judy asked.

Darcy shook her head no. She left Stan's side and continued through the kitchen. Judy looked at Trevor and he nodded for her to follow Darcy into the bedroom. She did, and closed the door behind them.

"Is she okay, Stan?" Trevor asked.

"She is one hurt and angry lady. I think she'll be fine. But it's going to take a while. One thing is for certain, you need to keep her away from that church out there. It's killing her. I'd go down and talk to Dave myself, but I know how independent churches feel about their autonomy. It wouldn't do a bit of good. That whole church autonomy thing is a myth, and simply serves to hide control. I don't know how you can be one church in a vacuum and not even want to talk to anybody else. Crazy."

"I need to head out, son," Woody said. "I've got a festival to get to. But if you need anything, you let me know, okay?"

"Okay, Woody. Thanks." Trevor gave the old man a hug.

"Just so you know, I haven't forgotten that you lost a daughter too."

"Thanks, Woody," Trevor said.

After Woody left, Ben and Kevin followed close behind. Trevor, Doc, and Stan sat at the table and chatted for a while before Judy came out of the bedroom, closing the door behind her.

"Well, she changed clothes and is in bed. She looked exhausted, so I think she's going to sleep for a while."

"She hasn't eaten in days as far as I know," Trevor said. "Certainly not much, anyway."

"I guess we need to head out too if we're going to get you to the airport," Stan said, looking at Doc. "I know it isn't your thing, Trev, but if you want to come visit me down at the church, you're welcome anytime. For right now, you might want to think about giving Darcy her space. This thing has become kind of personal between her and God now. Just check in with her occasionally. She can't feel abandoned either."

At the festival the following year, Trevor went but he went alone. He was driving his car when Judy, who was walking near the main entrance, saw him and waved. He pulled over next to her and rolled down the window.

"Hey Trev. Good to see you. You couldn't talk her into it, huh?" Judy asked.

"No," Trevor said. "I think we're done. I just came over to get away from it. The only time she comes out of the music room is when Rick brings the twins over to visit."

"Is she playing?" Judy asked.

"Heavens no. She just sits in there and reads and sleeps. I try to talk to her, but it ends up in a fight. You would think I pushed Dawn off that motorcycle myself. I'm going to go park over at our campsite for a while. It's paid for, so I may as well use it. I'll leave the car there and walk around. I don't know what else to do."

"Ben and Kevin pitched a tent over in rough camping. I'm sure they're around somewhere," Judy said. "Do you want to try to play a show, or do you want me to tell Jimmy to take us off the lineup?"

"I didn't even bring my banjo," Trevor said. "I really don't feel up to it."

"Don't worry about it. I'll talk to Jimmy." Judy patted his arm before he drove away.

Trevor drove to the old campsite, parked the car and got out. He looked around at the emptiness. There was nothing to set up. There was nothing there but his memories of the good times he had with his family. He put his hands in his pockets and started walking across the field to the vendor area, hoping to run into someone he knew—anyone.

He walked by Woody's place, but he hadn't set up shop yet, so Trevor continued walking down toward Preacher Stan's camp. As he approached it, he saw Woody and Doc sitting there and chatting with Stan.

"Hey Woody, Doc. How are you guys doing?"

"Well, looky here," Woody said as he and Doc stood up to shake Trevor's hand.

"Hey Preacher! How are ya?"

"Just fine, Trev," Stan said, standing up. "The question is, how are you?" He reached his hand out to take Trevor's.

"I've had better days," Trevor said.

"Grab a seat," Stan said. "Want some coffee or something?"

"That would be great."

Trevor pulled a lawn chair into the circle under the canopy. Stan went to the table set up on the side of the motorhome and poured a cup of coffee. "Black, right?"

"Yes sir."

Stan handed the cup to Trevor and sat back down. Sue, Stan's wife, stepped down out of the motorhome. "Hey, Trevor. How are you doin', hon? I was so sorry to hear about your loss last year."

"Thanks, Sue. I'm fine. Good to see ya." Trevor stood to give her a hug and sat back down.

Sue looked at Stan. "I'm gonna go spend some of your money." Then she turned to walk away. "You boys stay as long as you like. I'll leave you to solve the world's problems."

"See ya, Sue," Doc said.

"So how's our little Darcy doing? Will she be over here soon?" Woody asked. "I wanted to show her a new line of bows I just started carrying."

"No, Woody. She didn't come this time. She stayed home," Trevor said.

"What?" the three said almost in unison.

"She just isn't feeling well. I didn't even bring the motorhome. I probably won't stay long myself."

As they were talking, they heard a ruckus out on the road and all three turned to look. It was Ben, Kevin, and Jack Hanford walking together, laughing and slapping each other on the back.

"Hey, Trevor," Kevin yelled as soon as he saw him. "Good to see you, man. You guys want a funnel cake?" The three men laughed.

"Uh, no. None for me, thanks, Kev," Doc said.

Jack walked a little closer to the canopy. "Hey, Trevor. I'm really sorry for your loss, man."

"Thanks, Jack."

"Is Darcy doing okay?"

"She's fine, Jack."

Jack dropped his head and turned to walk back to the others. They continued with their stories and their walk to the funnel cake trailer.

Back home, Darcy was lying on the couch in the music room, one arm resting on her forehead. She had a book lying across her chest. There was a loud knock on the back door, and then she heard it open. "Nana. Nana, we're here!"

Darcy threw her feet off the couch and rocked up to a sitting position, trying to tame her hair and wipe her eyes to look presentable. She was still wearing a t-shirt and flannel pajama bottoms.

"Hey, girls," she said as she walked out of the music room and into the kitchen. "Hey, Rick, honey. How are you doing?"

"I'm fine. The girls wanted to see you. I hope you don't mind."

"Of course not. You're welcome to leave them here if you have stuff you need to do. You girls want to hang out with me today?"

"Yeah!" they shouted. "Can you teach me some more tunes on the fiddle?" Tracy Lynn asked.

Darcy looked up at Rick, confused.

"That's all she's been talking about lately," he said.

"Well, I'll tell you what. You girls stay in here and make us some sandwiches, and I'm going to go jump in the shower. After lunch, we'll all go in the music room and see what we can come up with."

Alison opened the refrigerator and started digging for meat and cheese while Tracy Lynn went to the cabinet for plates and glasses. Darcy stood and hugged Rick, kissing him on the cheek.

"Thank you, son," she said. "I really needed this today. You have a good day, okay?"

"I do have a few things to take care of. Thanks for letting them hang out. They love it here, you know."

Darcy smiled and patted Rick on the shoulder before he made his way out through the kitchen door.

"Bye, Daddy," the girls said.

Later that evening, Trevor returned home and heard some fiddling going on in the music room when he entered the back door. He knew it wasn't Darcy. He smiled when he realized that the twins were there.

He stuck his head in the door. "Hey there, girls."

"Papaw," Alison yelled. She jumped up and threw her arms around his waist, pressing her head on his stomach.

"I thought I heard some fiddling in here, Trevor said."

"It was Tracy Lynn," Alison said.

"Well, Tracy Lynn is sounding real good, I'd say."

Tracy Lynn handed the fiddle and bow to Darcy, and got up to hug Trevor.

"How was the festival?" Darcy asked.

"I don't know. Just isn't the same. I think I'm going to go stay at Stan and Sue's place tonight. He gave me his house key."

Darcy looked at him with her sad, swollen eyes. Trevor felt a pang in his heart. Was this it? Was everything over? He waited for Darcy to say something, anything, but she only nodded, holding back her tears.

"I just can't," he said. "Okay, girls, you have a good time with Nana. I have to leave again, but I'll see you soon, okay?"

"Okay, Papaw. I love you," Alison said.

She and Tracy Lynn were still wrapping themselves around Trevor's waist.

"How about you girls go in the kitchen and pour us something to drink?" Darcy said.

They ran out of the room as Darcy laid the fiddle and bow aside. "They don't have a clue what's going on," she said.

"Well, that's good, I guess. Are they missing their mom?"

"Yes. Of course. They wanted to hear stories about her and Tracy earlier. They're trying to cope like everyone else. They're pretty strong little girls."

"Well, I'm going to go pack some things. I'll be back in a few days for the rest."

"Trevor, I'm sorry I've been such a terrible wife."

"You haven't been a terrible wife. But you won't let me near you to try to help, and I can't sit around and watch you put yourself though this any longer."

"I know," Darcy said, lowering her eyes to the floor.

Trevor left.

CHAPTER 11

Gratitude

"Gratitude unlocks the fullness of life. It turns what we have into enough, and more. It turns denial into acceptance, chaos to order, confusion to clarity. It can turn a meal into a feast, a house into a home, a stranger into a friend."
~ Melody Beattie

Judy was straightening up the kitchen in her motorhome while Tom sat sideways in the driver's seat, looking at some brochures. A shadow moved across the window outside and caught Judy's eye.

"It's Darcy!" she shouted. Judy wiped her hands and rushed out the door. "Hey, girl."

"Hey," Darcy said as she sat on the picnic table.

"Did you just get here?" Judy leaned over to give Darcy a hug.

"I did. I thought I might give it a try this year."

"Well, the place sure hasn't been the same without you the last couple years."

"I've missed everyone so much," Darcy said.

"Want some coffee?"

"Sure."

Still talking, Judy climbed back inside. "How are those twins doing?"

"Hi, Darcy!" Tom yelled from inside the motorhome.

"Hey, Tom!" Judy was banging around inside, looking for a cup. "The twins are fine," she said. "They came with me. They're walking around over there in the vendor area."

"That's great. How fun that'll be. I bet they're getting so big," Judy said through the open window looking out over the sink.

"Oh, they are—and just as beautiful as their momma."

"We saw Trevor a little while ago. He got his motorhome set up last night. Have you seen him?"

Darcy pulled her jacket collar up around her cheeks and looked out across the campground, her long hair shimmering in the gentle breeze. Judy kicked open the door and stepped down with a cup in each hand.

"I haven't seen him. We haven't really spoken in almost two years."

"Really?" Judy handed a cup to Darcy and sat in a lawn chair next to the picnic table.

"Yeah. Poor Rick. Any communicating that needs done, we do through him, pretty much. He's been great. Like everything, the girls just take it in stride."

"He isn't still living with Stan, is he?"

"Oh no. He only did that for a couple weeks. He has an apartment in town."

"Don't you miss him?"

"I miss the memory of him. The good times we had. The great music we played together. But I haven't been able to get past the anger."

"Honey, you have to know that Dawn's death wasn't his fault."

"Judy, he loved that motorcycle as much as Rick did. That's all they talked about. It made me so mad that he always encouraged her to go riding all the time." She paused. "Oh, never mind. I don't really want to talk about it."

"So, where are you going to stay?" Judy asked.

"Believe it or not, me and the girls pitched a tent over in rough camping."

"Really? That sounds like fun."

"Oh yeah. We're going to have a regular two-day slumber party. I've been working with Tracy Lynn on the fiddle. It's so adorable to see how quickly she picks it up. Alison is her biggest fan. Watching those two together is like watching Tracy and Dawn. It melts my heart."

"Nice. I'm glad she's playing. What about you? You play much?"

"Not really. Just enough to teach her."

"What ever happened to Weiser?"

Darcy thought for a few minutes, sipping on her coffee. "Weiser. Now there's a name I haven't thought about in years."

"Sweetie, that was what your heart pumped blood for. It was your dream."

"I know. I know. I don't know why I put so much effort into such a silly thing. That all seems so far away now. It just isn't that important."

"Well, I guess," Judy said. "You guys come over for supper later, if you want."

"That sounds really good. He isn't going to be here, is he?"

"I don't think so. I wouldn't worry about it. You'll have the girls to do the talking, if need be."

They giggled and sipped on their coffee.

"I need to go talk to Woody," Darcy said. "Have you seen him yet?"

"No, not yet. But I'm sure he's over there."

"Okay. I'll catch up after a while."

"All right, sweetie. We'll be here."

"See ya, Tom!" Darcy yelled into the motorhome.

"Bye, Darcy."

She handed her empty cup to Judy, got up from the picnic table, and started walking down the gravel lane toward the vendor area. As she neared the fence line, she glanced at the field and saw a couple deer. "Still there," she thought.

"Weiser. God, Weiser." Her thoughts drifted off to the fiddle contest. She saw herself on the stage and heard the audience cheering. It was such a familiar scene to her, but she hadn't been there in a while. It was comforting. She kept walking, the willow trees that lined the fence offering her shade. She turned her head to follow the deer, paying no attention to where she was walking.

"Nana!"

She was startled from her daydream, and turned to see the twins running toward her. They were each holding tightly to a paper plate covered in powdered sugar with a funnel cake barely visible underneath.

"What in the world have you got?" she said, knowing full well what they were.

"Funnel cakes," Tracy Lynn said with a sinister grin.

"Let me guess. You ran into Ben and Kevin over there."

The girls chuckled. "Uncle Ben bought 'em for us," Alison said.

"Of course he did. I'm headed up there to see Mister Woody. You girls wanna go?"

They nodded and each took a bite, turning to follow Darcy. They walked around the curve at the end of the fence line and Darcy heard a jam session in the distance. Her heart sank when she recognized Trevor's banjo playing. She could always tell his playing with a blindfold on, from a mile away.

"Is that your Papaw up there playing?"

"Yeah, we talked to him earlier," Alison said.

They continued their stroll down the lane, and Darcy looked back and forth at all the campsites, waiting to see anyone she knew. The twins had powdered sugar all over their faces as they tried to walk and talk and eat at the same time.

"You guys need to slow down," Darcy said.

Tracy Lynn started giggling, and then Alison burst out laughing. She spat a cloud of white powder and doubled over coughing. She laughed until tears rolled down her cheek. Darcy stopped and turned around to look at them. "Oh, good grief," she said. "I told you."

Then Darcy started laughing at the girls. Tracy Lynn was pointing at Alison, but by then she was laughing too hard to say anything. All three stood in the middle of the lane, bent over, laughing.

Trevor, who had just finished playing, looked over to see what the ruckus was all about. He saw who it was and smiled at the laughter. It was good to hear her laugh again, he thought. He watched as Tracy Lynn took the paper plate from Alison and carried it, along with hers, over to a trash can on the edge of the lane. The girls, still laughing, brushed the powder from their hands and faces as they headed toward the vendor area. Darcy glanced over and saw Trevor looking at them. She smiled and nodded, but kept walking. Trevor returned the nod, and then turned back around to rejoin the circle for the next tune.

"Mister Woody," the twins shouted as they ran toward his workbench. He was draped in his usual denim apron with pencils stuck in the top pockets, saw dust and wood shavings all over it. But the girls didn't mind.

"Look who we have here," Woody said as both of the girls wrapped their arms around his waist. "Hey there, sweetie," he said as Darcy walked into his arms.

"It's so good to see you, Woody. It's always like coming home to grandpa."

"Oh. Well, alrighty then." He blushed. "Hey, Tracy Lynn, there's a fiddle over there around the corner that you might like to try out."

The girls nodded and ran away.

"Wait, wait," Darcy shouted. "How about you two run over there to the shower house and wash your face and hands first?"

They giggled and ran across the lane.

"Those girls," Darcy said, turning back to Woody.

"How have you been, Darcy?" he asked.

"I've been doing pretty good," she said. "Getting better, a little at a time."

"Well, that's good. It's in the right direction, I reckon."

"Yeah. It's just hard when I think that I've lost everything. My girls. My marriage. My dreams. Everything."

"Let's have a seat over here, honey."

Woody reached up to the edge of his canopy and turned the *closed* sign around, and then he spun a lawn chair around to sit in front of Darcy. "So, you think you've lost everything?"

"Pretty much."

"Look there," Woody said, pointing to the twins walking back from the shower house.

They were chatting and smiling as they went around the corner to the tent where the special fiddle was. They didn't even glance back at Darcy and Woody. Darcy watched them until they were out of sight.

"You know what I think will help?" Woody said.

"What's that?" Darcy asked.

"I think you need to do a better job focusing on gratitude."

"What do you mean?"

"Paying attention to what you do have," he said. "Honey, you're so focused on the two girls you've lost, you don't see the blessing of those two girls right in front of you."

"I love those girls more than anything," Darcy said, tears welling up in her eyes.

"I know you do, hon. That's my point. They are just the beginning. You have so much to be grateful for, but you never take the time to look around and recognize it."

She paused for a minute as she thought about it. "And I have dear friends like you," she said.

"And you have dear friends like me," he laughed. The sound of a fiddle danced from around the corner. "Wow! You've been working with her."

"Yes. She's doing really well."

"Yes, she is," Woody said.

They sat listening for a few minutes to Tracy Lynn tuning a little and playing a little.

"She's finicky, like her Nana. That's good."

Darcy smiled and kicked Woody's foot.

"You know what you might do?" Woody said. "You might start keeping a journal so you can write down the things you're grateful for. That way it comes more alive for you. It keeps things in front of you. Do you have a journal?"

"No. I just don't know what I would write. There isn't that much..."

"Honey, look around you. Look at these trees. Look at the sky. The air you breathe. The food you eat. Each morning you get to wake up."

Darcy's eyes got big as she sat up straight in the chair. "Oh, you mean that. I hadn't really thought of it all like that."

"Most of us don't," he said. "But sweetheart, there's one thing you really need to think a lot about, and get it in that journal."

"What's that?" she asked.

"The gifts that God entrusted you with. What are you doing with them?"

Darcy lowered her gaze to the ground and fell silent, listening to the beautiful waltz coming from around the corner. She saw herself playing that same tune years earlier, when she was Tracy Lynn's age.

After a few minutes, the music stopped and the twins reappeared. Tracy Lynn's eyes were big with excitement as she walked over to Woody.

"That is really nice," she said. "How much allowance would I need to save up to get something like that?"

"That one might take a while," Woody said.

Darcy smiled at him, and then looked at Tracy Lynn. "I don't think there are enough chores in the world to cover the cost of that fiddle."

"Nana, can we go back over there where Papaw is and listen to them play?" Alison asked.

"Of course, honey."

"There's a case for that fiddle over there under the table. Why don't you take it with you?" Woody said.

"Really? Are you sure?" Tracy Lynn asked.

"Yes, I'm sure. You can bring it back when you're done jamming. Just take good care of it."

"Oh, I will," Tracy Lynn said before she and Alison ran back around the corner, full of excitement.

Darcy's jaw dropped. "Are you sure about this?"

"Well yes," Woody said. "She isn't going to hurt it. If she was trained by anyone other than you, I might be a little more skeptical. But caring for an instrument is nothing I'm worried about with your bunch."

"That's really sweet, Woody. Thank you. I think you have a friend for life there."

"We'll see you later, Nana," Alison said, reappearing with Tracy Lynn.

"Don't run with that," Darcy warned.

"I won't," Tracy Lynn shouted over her shoulder.

Darcy smiled as she watched the twins walk slowly down the lane. She sensed Woody watching her as she stared at the girls.

"You look star struck," he said.

She chuckled. "I guess I am. Those two never cease to amaze me."

She turned to Woody, and then gazed out across the lane and into the campground. "You're right, Woody. I have so much to be grateful for."

"We all do, sweetie. Have you talked to Trevor yet?"

"Oh, no. There's nothing to talk about, really. Since the divorce, we just don't seem to have anything connecting us, except those girls, of course. They make sure we don't get too far apart. It was kind of funny, last night, when we were packing, Alison asked me if I didn't like Papaw anymore."

"I bet that got interesting."

"It did. I told her that of course I still loved him. We raised their mom and their aunt together. You just don't forget all that. I think they may be getting genuinely concerned about it."

"I'm sure they are."

"Hey, Woody," a voice came from the lane.

Woody turned. "Hey, Jack."

Jack Hanford came into view. "Well hello there, Darcy."

"Hey, Jack." She dropped her sunglasses from the top of her head back down to her nose.

"Woody, can I get you to take a look at the frets on my guitar after while? The bottom ones might be getting close to needing replaced. I want to see what you think."

"Sure. Bring it by anytime. I'll be here."

"Thanks. I'll see you in a bit. See ya around, Darcy."

"Uh huh," she groaned.

Woody and Darcy sat quietly until Jack rounded the curve.

"He really is an awesome guitar player. Even Ben knows it," Woody said.

"Is there a point there?" Darcy smiled.

"Well, I guess I just don't understand why you two stay so crossways all the time."

"I guess we just got off on the wrong foot. It's a mutual thing, really. He doesn't like classically trained fiddlers and I don't much care for arrogant asses."

Woody laughed.

"I guess I'll head over and see who's selling what this year, then go back to the tent for a while," Darcy said.

"You're in a tent?"

"Yeah, we're roughing it this time. It's fun, though."

"I suppose," Woody said.

Darcy slapped him on the knee as she stood. "Thanks for the chat, Woody. I'll see you around."

"Okay, sweetie. Don't be a stranger."

Darcy walked down the line of vendors knowing everything would be the same as it had always been. She thought about all the cheap jewelry, tuners, t-shirts, cassette tapes, and CDs she had bought here through the years. She stopped at a t-shirt table and looked at this year's design for the festival. Always different. Always too busy. It never failed. Whoever did the design always seemed to want to list the bands or some other detail, as if people were going to stand in front of you and read your stomach or behind you to read your back. She giggled to herself and moved on.

She strolled across the lane, heading in the opposite direction to check out the vendors on the other side. She smiled at the carnival trailers with the cotton candy, ice cream, and funnel cake signs, adorned with blinking lights.

As she strolled past one of the canopied tables, she noticed some stationery supplies. She had seen this table before, but she never really paid attention to it. She usually just walked by. But this time was different. Next to the pens, envelopes, and cards, she saw a stack of rustic-looking hardback books. "Are these journals?" she asked.

"Yes, ma'am," the young girl said. "We have some lined ones and some blank ones. I think we might even have some with the gridlines back in these boxes somewhere."

Darcy picked one up and flipped through it. She kept thinking about Woody and his suggestion to start a journal. After looking through several of them, she picked one that was a soft leather bound, plush dark material with a tie string around it and silk ribbon page marker in the middle. She held it in her left hand, and then her right. She flipped through the pages over and over, and rubbed the cover. Then she sniffed its rich smell. "I really like this one," she said. "I'll take this and a couple of those pens over there."

"Yes, ma'am. That'll be twenty-six dollars." The young girl handed Darcy a bag and took the money from her.

Darcy turned and walked away with a smile, still thinking of Woody. As she strolled back to the tent, she noticed that things seemed a little brighter. She looked back and forth from one side of the lane to the other, watching all of the people and hearing a number of distant jam sessions off in various directions. She noticed kids laughing and running around, playing tag, or playing with cheap toys their parents had just bought them.

She saw a small boy with an ice cream cone, chocolate all over the front of his little *Festival of the Bluegrass* t-shirt. She gazed up into the sky, shook her long blonde hair in the breeze, down over her back, and walked a little faster—a little taller.

Under a canopy of tree boughs, Darcy sauntered into the deep shade of the woods. This was the rough camping area where there were hundreds of tents. But she had managed to find a secluded corner where she pitched hers away from any noise. She rolled back the front flaps and tied them, slid off her shoes, and climbed in.

She sat on some of the quilts that covered the floor, and moved pillows around to get comfortable. She took the journal and pens from the bag. She got quiet and waited for thoughts to come to her. She stared out of the door into the woods, recalling her friends and how they had helped her. "What am I really grateful for?" she said under her breath.

Her friends' faces started going through her mind as she remembered the many conversations they'd had since Tracy died, and then again when Dawn died. "They really have been such good friends," she said to herself.

She started writing. The more she wrote, the more the memories flooded back to her. She sat writing for hours, shifting in the pillows and blankets occasionally. They seemed like minutes. She laughed. She cried. She got angry. But most of all, she wrote.

After many pages were filled, she thought of the conversation she had had with Judy about empathy. She wrote the word in big letters.

EMPATHY.

"I need to put myself in the shoes of others instead of getting angry with them. Their experiences brought them to where they are," she wrote.

The discussion she had had with Doc about attitude came to mind. Again, she wrote the word in large block letters.

ATTITUDE.

"People can only hurt me if I choose to be hurt. They only make an impact in my life to the extent that I choose to let them. I can live life with regret, or I can live life with joy and a vision for the future. An attitude of forgiveness can change the world."

Then she wrote,

DEVOTION.

It was the conversation she had had with Preacher Stan. "I have to commit myself to the people and things I love. I also have to recognize the need for God in my life and stay devoted to Him."

Finally, the conversation she had just had with Woody was about...

GRATITUDE.

"Even after all of the loss and pain, I still have so much to be grateful for. The essentials of life. My beautiful granddaughters. And I need to start being more respectful of the gifts God has entrusted to me. How awful that I thought I could live without them."

She stopped writing. Darcy set the journal down on her lap and laid the pen aside. She stared at the four words she had highlighted, repeating them over and over again.

"Empathy. Attitude. Devotion. Gratitude. Empathy. Attitude. Devotion. Gratitude."

She knew she needed to remember these key ideas that she got from her friends, so she went back and underlined the first letters. E A D G. After a short minute of staring at her notes, she smiled. Then she laughed. Then she roared out loud and fell over backwards.

"Of course!" She shouted. "E. A. D. G."

E, A, D, and G are the notes of the strings on her fiddle. What better way to remember what her friends had helped her focus on? She continued to laugh until tears ran down her face. And then she cried. She knew God was writing his will on her heart. She had known it for a long time but hid it away. She looked around the tent, laughing and crying and laughing again.

"Hey, what's going on in there?" It was Ben and Kevin.

"Oh, crap," she said, still laughing.

"You okay?" Kevin asked.

"I'm fine. I'm fine," she said, giggling and wiping her face as she climbed out of the tent.

"You sure?" Ben asked.

"Really. I'm fine. It's nothing."

They all hugged, and then they sat in the lawn chairs surrounding the small fire pit.

"How did you know where I was?" Darcy asked.

"Well, imagine our surprise when Woody told us you were here and that you were staying in a tent," Kevin said. "Are you kidding? A tent?"

"It's fun. The girls love it. Besides, you two are staying in a tent."

"Yeah. But we're…us," Ben said. "We just saw Tracy Lynn over there playing with Trevor and whoever that is he's jamming with. She's impressing the heck out of everybody over there."

"She's doing really well," Darcy said. "She reminds me so much of her Aunt Tracy."

"No campfire?" Kevin said.

"Not yet. I'm sure the girls will start one later. We're equipped for s'mores. Hey, Ben, do you think I can be ready for Weiser by next year?"

Ben started laughing. "What? June? Where did that come from?"

"What are you saying?" Kevin looked at Ben and back at Darcy.

"Well, I just kinda had a little chat with God, I think. This thing on my heart almost climbed up out of my throat."

The three of them laughed.

"Are you sure about this?" Ben asked.

"I am."

The three of them sat and began making plans for Weiser. "You'll need some stage time," Ben said. "You know, to get some practice in front of judges."

"Yes. I think I'll go back to Athens in October, and maybe a couple more nearby in the spring," Darcy said.

"You're really going to do it, huh?" Ben asked.

"I have to. Will you go and back me up on your guitar?"

"Of course I will. It'll be a blast."

CHAPTER 12

Winning

*"Many people die with their music still in them. Why is this so?
Too often it is because they are always getting ready to live.
Before they know it, time runs out."*
~ Oliver Wendell Holmes

Darcy walked around Weiser High School with her fiddle strapped to her back. She saw a few other musicians but was clearly lost.

"Where's all the jamming?" she asked of one of the people walking by with a guitar case in his hand.

"Stickerville," he said. "You need to check out Stickerville."

"Where's... that?" she asked, turning as he walked away from her. He didn't even slow down. "Stickerville," she said to herself. She continued to walk around the school parking lot trying to get the lay of the land.

"First time here?"

Darcy turned to see a sweet old man talking to her. He smiled at her through his aged white goatee, and he wore a black Irish cabbie hat.

"Yes, sir. Yes, it is." She smiled. "Do I look lost?"

"Well, maybe a little. Can I help you find anything?" he said.

"Actually, I was just curious where all the jamming is. I wanted to look things over and kill some time. Someone I spoke to mentioned Stickerville, but didn't have time to tell me where it is."

"Yes, there's Stickerville, but there's also what they call Fiddletown. It's a campground around there behind the high school. Stickerville is across the road, behind that line of old buildings. A lot of people like it there. I don't care for it myself, but you might like it. Some folks refer to the two lovingly, as the high-rent district and the low-rent district."

"I see. Do you know where I go to register for the competition?" Darcy asked.

"Oh, my. You're a competition fiddler, then?"

"Well, yes. I suppose you could say that. I've never played here, but I thought I might give it a try. It's been a long time coming. My name is Darcy Marshall, by the way."

"Charlie. Charlie O'Flynn," the old man said, reaching his hand out to take hers. "You can call me Charlie."

"Well, it's a pleasure meeting you, Charlie."

"You as well, my dear. The registration tables are in there in the foyer. They can probably answer all of your questions, too. Where do you hail from?"

"I came out from Eastern Kentucky, near Prestonsburg."

"I see. That's where they grow horses and fiddlers, eh?"

"Why, yes, I suppose it is," she said with a smile.

"Did you come out by yourself?" Charlie asked.

"I did, but I'm supposed to meet some friends here that are coming from other parts of the country. In fact, my guitar player is supposed to be here already. His name is Ben Salinger. I don't suppose you've seen an equally lost guitar player?"

"No, I haven't. But I'm sure he'll be along. I need to go inside, my dear. Did you want to go in with me and check in?"

"Uh, sure. I'll go in."

The two walked into the side entrance of the high school where there were tables lined up in the foyer. It looked like a trophy room. There were a couple ladies sitting behind the tables with binders full of paper forms and applications in front of them.

"Hello there, Charlie," one of the ladies called out. Her loud voice echoed through the halls of the facility.

"Mornin', Marie," he said. "This here is Darcy, all the way from Kentucky, and she needs to get her bearings. Can you help her out?"

"Of course we can," Marie said, smiling at Darcy.

Darcy returned the smile and patted Charlie on the back. "Darcy Marshall," she said, returning Marie's smile.

"Let's see here," Marie said, as she flipped through the papers in one of the large binders.

"I was hoping to meet a gentleman named Ben Salinger here. Has he checked in?"

"Is he playing with you?"

"Yes, ma'am."

"Okay. He would still be listed with you then. Let's see here. Yes. Here you are. But no, he hasn't been here yet. You won out at Athens?"

"Yes, I did."

"Well, congratulations. There's no entry fee for sanctioned winners. I've got you checked off. Melinda there has your VIP Pass and a lanyard to hang it around your neck. Here's a schedule for the festival. The competition times will be posted back in that waiting room there once everyone has checked in."

"Okay. Thank you," Darcy said. She collected her pass and lanyard and walked with Charlie down the hall a short distance to look into the darkened gymnasium.

"So that's where it happens, huh?"

"That's it, my dear."

"Unbelievable. I feel like I've made the journey to Mecca."

"Yep. Pretty much," Charlie said with a chuckle.

"Hey, girl," a familiar voice said. "I thought you might be in here."

Darcy turned. "Judy!" Their voices and footsteps echoed through the halls as they joined up in a giggly embrace. "I am so glad to see you," Darcy said. "I'm starting to freak out a little that Ben isn't here."

"Relax, it'll be fine, Judy said. "Who have we here?"

The old man smiled and took his hat off.

"This here is my new friend, Mr. Charlie O'Flynn, Darcy said. He's been showing me the ropes."

"Well, hello, Mr. Charlie O'Flynn," Judy repeated. "I'm pleased to meet you."

"You as well, my dear," he said, reaching for her hand.

"Thank you for taking care of my friend here," Judy said.

"It's been my pleasure indeed," Charlie said. "But, I'll leave you two now. I have work to do."

"Okay, Charlie. We'll see you around, okay?" Darcy said.

"Yes. Yes, you will," he said as he walked down the hallway and out of sight.

"He's an interesting old guy," Judy said.

"He's been such a sweetheart," Darcy said. "He told me there's some jamming going on over in a campground close by. You think Ben might be over there?"

"With him, anything is possible," Judy said, shaking her head.

"True."

Darcy waved as she and Judy walked toward the doors. "We'll see you soon, ladies."

"Okay, Miss Marshall," Marie said. "Have fun."

Darcy and Judy walked through the doors, out into the parking lot.

"Looks like a lot of people going around there," Judy said, gesturing toward the street past the running track.

"I just hope he's in there," Darcy said.

"Will you relax? He'll be here. By the way, where's the rest of your stuff?" Judy asked.

"Oh, it's locked up in the back of my rental car. I just didn't want to leave my fiddle in there."

Darcy and Judy walked in front of the baseball diamond and around the curve toward the makeshift campground. Across the street were several charming old block buildings, one with a red sign next to the road that read, NATIONAL OLDTIME FIDDLERS CONTEST & FESTIVAL HEADQUARTERS.

"Amazing," Darcy said.

"What?"

"I still can't believe I'm actually here."

"Oh, you're here all right," Judy said. "I'm just tickled to be here with you."

Darcy spun around a few times, her arms spread out wide, taking in all there was to see. When they finally made it to the Fiddletown campground, there was a line of people checking in. Darcy started looking for Ben.

"Can we go on in?" Judy asked one of the men at the table. "We aren't staying. Just looking for someone."

"Sure. Go on in," the man said.

The two strolled up and down the rows of campers, weaving in and out of stacks of supplies as people were getting organized. They saw a few jam sessions already starting.

"Look. Look. There's Kevin," Darcy said. She pointed across the field where they saw a standup bass in a circle of musicians. They made their way through the crowds and the tents, and finally made it to Kevin's jam. When he saw them coming, he smiled but kept playing. The girls stopped at the edge of the circle. Darcy finally took the time to pay attention to the musicians.

"Holy cow. These guys are good," she said, leaning into Judy. As soon as the tune ended, they walked around the circle to greet Kevin.

"Hey there," he said, leaning away from his bass to give them each a hug. "So good to see you guys."

"You too," Darcy said. "You all sound great."

"I have no idea who these people are," he giggled.

"Have you seen Ben?" Darcy asked.

"No, not yet. I really thought he would have been here by now."

"Well, I'm freaking out," she said. "I can't do this without a guitar player and I really wanted to go over some stuff with him tonight. Round one for the Grand Champion Division starts tomorrow evening."

"Say what?" Kevin said. "You aren't playing with the Seniors?"

"Shut up," Darcy said, giving Kevin a backhand to his stomach. She glanced at Judy and rolled her eyes. They all laughed.

"No, really. You're going for the big kahuna right off the bat?"

"Kevin, I've been anticipating this 'big kahuna' all my life."

"I suppose. These judges don't know you, though."

"Well, I'll just have to work harder. We're going to look around some more," Darcy said. "We'll catch up with you later on."

"Okie-dokie." Kevin went back to join the circle.

Darcy and Judy headed back toward the entrance gate, walking past the crowds, and searched for Ben. By the time they had gotten back on the road, Darcy was staring at the ground, deep in thought. "This could be bad. This could be really bad," she said.

"Let's go back around to the school. Maybe there's a phone there you can use," Judy said.

When they arrived in the foyer, Darcy asked Marie if there was a phone available. She pointed down the hall behind the tables toward the entrance to the auditorium that was housed in the same building, next to the gym.

They rushed to the phone booth and Darcy dialed Ben's number. When he answered the phone, her jaw dropped and tears pooled in her eyes. "Ben?"

"Oh no," Judy whispered, turning away from Darcy, putting her hand to her forehead.

"Ben, what's going on? Why aren't you here?" Darcy asked.

After what seemed like an eternity, Judy looked at Darcy, motioning for an answer.

"Oh, God. I know, I know. It isn't your fault," Darcy said. "Is there a chance you can make it tomorrow?"

Judy endured another pause, waiting impatiently, for some kind of an answer.

"I understand. Yes, I understand. Okay. Bye."

"What in the heck is going on?" Judy said as Darcy hung up the phone.

Darcy started crying and leaned her head against the side of the phone booth. Judy rubbed her back, waiting for her to catch her breath.

"What, honey?"

"They had some kind of crisis where he works. He doesn't know when he's going to be here, if at all. He said he didn't know how to get in touch with me or he would have told me sooner."

They went outside. Darcy sat on the bench of a picnic table, almost falling down. Judy sat next to her and put her arm around Darcy, where they stayed in silence for several minutes.

"Now what?" Judy asked.

"I wish I knew. I don't understand," Darcy said, still wiping the tears from her face. "Why would God bring me all the way out here, and then this?" She took the fiddle off of her back and laid it behind her on the table. She leaned back on her elbows and looked into the sky. "Why, Lord?"

Judy also leaned back on her elbows, and followed Darcy's gaze. She peeked at Darcy and back at the sky. "Better say something here, God," she said. "This little girl here is pissed."

Darcy smiled, but kept staring up into the deep blue sky. Then she closed her eyes. Judy closed her eyes too, both of them letting the morning sun warm their sorrowful faces. Several minutes passed. Then...

"Well, hello there."

They both opened their eyes with a jolt and looked down simultaneously.

"Jack?" Darcy said.

"Oh no!" Judy started laughing.

"Jack, what are you doing here?" Darcy asked.

"I'm always here. I've been coming to these things for years."

"Are you serious?" Darcy asked. She looked over at Judy. Judy looked back at her. They busted out laughing as Jack looked on.

"Was it something I said? Do I have something in my nose?" Jack asked.

They laughed even harder while wiping their tears—this time, tears of joy.

"Jack, this is unbelievable. Have you ever played at one of these contests?" Darcy asked.

"I've backed up a lot of fiddlers here through the years. Yes."

Darcy shook her head. "Unbelievable."

Then she asked, "Jack, do you think you could bring yourself to back up a classically trained blonde chick, who doesn't belong in this music?"

He chuckled. "I'd love to. It would be an honor. But I'm surprised you're asking me."

She dropped her head again, smiling and sniffing.

"Thank you," she whispered, looking into the sky.

"I had no idea you even liked old-time music," Darcy said.

"I'm guessing you really know little about me," he said.

Darcy and Judy looked at each other. "True," they said together and chuckled.

"When can we get together to practice?" Darcy asked.

"I've got my fifth-wheel set up at the far back corner of the campground over there. Why don't you guys come over in a couple hours and we'll figure it out."

"Okay, great," Darcy said.

Jack left as the girls sat dumbfounded. Judy shook her head. "What the heck just happened?" she asked.

"I don't know, but we better go tell Marie," Darcy said. They stood and Darcy put her fiddle case on her back and they went into the foyer.

"Hey, Marie," Darcy said.

"Hey, honey. What's up?"

"Marie, can I change my accompanist from Ben Salinger to Jack Hanford?"

"Jack's playing with you?" Marie asked.

"Why, yes. Do you know him?"

"Of course. Lucky you. Everybody here knows Jack. Been coming here for years."

Darcy leaned on the table and shook her head once again. Then she looked over at Judy. Judy shrugged her shoulders, smiled, and looked away.

"Sure, honey," Marie said. "Let me get that changed for you."

"Thank you. Where's the nearest place to eat? I'm starving."

"Well, if you go into town, there are lots of good places down there. If you want fast food, that's down there, too. You can take the shuttle bus if you like, or there's plenty of parking down there if you're driving."

"Okay. Thanks for all your help, Marie." Darcy and Judy left the school and drove into town.

When they finished eating, they went back up to the Fiddletown Campground. Walking through the crowds, Darcy and Judy ran into Kevin, still playing his bass in the same jam circle. Judy poked him in the side and startled him. He pulled away from the circle, dragging his bass along with him. "Hey," he said.

"Hey," Judy said. "Did you happen to see anyone here that you know?"

"No, why?"

"Well. Ben might not make it."

"Oh, no," he said, looking at Darcy.

"No problem," Darcy said, shrugging her shoulders. "It's covered."

"Huh?"

"You're never going to guess who's here," Judy said.

"Who?"

"Jack," Darcy said.

"Jack?" Kevin repeated with a puzzled look. "Jack Hanford?"

Both of the girls nodded their heads with a crooked grin.

"Jack is going to play with you?"

They nodded again.

"Are you serious?"

They continued to nod with an awkward grin, then they all started laughing.

"That's sweet," Kevin laughed. "I can't believe you, of all people, are actually going to play music with Jack Hanford."

"I didn't know what else to do," Darcy said. "Ben ran into some trouble at work and doesn't know if he's even going to be able to make it. Jack was really nice to us when we ran into him. He said he's been coming here for years. Apparently, everyone here knows him, and even likes him."

Kevin smiled and shook his head. "Amazing."

"We're headed over to his camp now to practice some. He said he's back there in the corner. You want to come with us?"

"I may be there later on. You guys go ahead."

When the two finally found Jack's fifth-wheel, there was no one around.

"Anybody here?" Judy shouted.

Darcy turned and hit her on the arm. "Will you shush?"

"Ouch. What? He invited us."

"Hey there," Jack said. "Make yourselves at home. I'll be right out."

Judy sat in a lawn chair while Darcy laid her fiddle case on a folding table that was sitting empty next to the camper. She opened it, set up her fiddle, and tightened her bow. As she tuned, Jack came out of the camper with his guitar.

"So, what's it going to be?" he asked.

Darcy rosined her bow while she named off some of her contest tunes. Jack passed judgment on each one of them.

"That won't work."

"Yep, that's a good one."

"No, better leave that one out."

"I think they might go for that one."

"Okay, that's annoying now," Darcy said.

"Well, I know most of these judges," Jack said. "...what they've heard a thousand times and what might be fresh for them."

"I suppose," she said.

After they had selected some tunes and practiced awhile, Jack went into the camper and brought out a pitcher of iced tea and some glasses.

"You guys want something to munch on?"

"Not me. I'm good," Judy said.

Darcy shook her head no.

Darcy and Jack worked late into the night on the eighteen tunes they would need to get through the competition. Each round needed to include a hoedown, a waltz, and then a tune in the style of the contestant's choice. Judy had left long before Darcy, and walked around the campground to find Kevin.

"Oh Lord, it's two o'clock," Darcy said.

"Yeah, my fingers are about shot for tonight," Jack said.

They both put their instruments away and sat back to finish their tea.

"You know, I was thinking about what you said earlier," Jack said. "When you saw me over in front of the school—about playing with a classically trained, blonde chick. You threw me there for a minute, but I remember when I said that now, and I am really sorry. I was such an idiot back in those days, pretty much intimidated by anyone with real talent. I guess I'm shocked that you remembered all that."

"Don't worry about it, Jack. Water under the bridge," Darcy said.

"Well, it does explain why you guys have never wanted anything to do with me."

"I'm just glad you're here to help me through this," she said. "You really are an awesome guitar player."

"Thanks. I think you've got a real shot at this," Jack said. "You're pretty awesome yourself."

"I'm just grateful to finally be here. I need to go find Judy and see if she's ready to go. I'm exhausted."

"Okay. See you in the morning, then?"

"Yep. Let's meet at our room. We're staying at the Colonial Motel. Say eight-thirty?"

"Sounds good. See you then."

With all of the practicing and the first five rounds throughout the week behind them, everything was going well for Darcy. Much to her amazement, she was still in the running for Grand Champion. Early Saturday afternoon, there was a knock at the door.

"Hello, boys," Judy said, swinging the door open. "Kevin and Jack are here!" she shouted.

"Oh, hey. Come on in. Grab a stale donut," Darcy said. Jack, I thought we were going to meet at the school.

"Me too, but I saw Kevin and just latched on."

"She's trying to teach herself how to breathe," Judy said, pointing at Darcy.

"Round 6. The finals. Unbelievable," Kevin said. "Still nothing from Ben?"

"No. I hate it that he won't be here for this, after all these years," Darcy said.

Darcy and Jack had started Thursday evening and made it all the way to the final round. Here she was playing at *The granddaddy of them all*, as she remembered her friends at the Conservatory calling it.

"It's time to roll," Jack said. "We need to get up there."

"Okay. Okay. Let's move," Judy said as they all crowded toward the door.

"Welcome to the final round of the National Grand Champion Fiddle Contest," the emcee announced. "You're going to witness some amazing talent here tonight."

"My God. Look," Darcy said, pointing at the side of the stage. "It's Charlie!"

"Good grief," Judy said. "Why didn't that old coot tell us he was the emcee tonight?"

"Beats me," Darcy said.

Darcy and Jack went into the waiting room. Darcy watched Judy and Kevin walk into the back of the gym. She knew Judy liked taking in the whole show when things like this happened, audience and all. There were only ten contestants left in the final round. After numbers were drawn, Darcy was number ten to play. They sat around on the tables in the makeshift greenroom and practiced their last three tunes. "This is going to be a long wait," she said to Jack as all the contestants in front of them played.

While in the "next up" seat, Darcy listened in awe of the musicians on stage right in front of her. Her attention kept flashing back and forth from the stage to the years that had gone by and all the things that she had experienced. She smiled when she remembered the first time Tracy played on stage in Lexington. She almost laughed out loud at the memory of Tracy and Dawn trying to cook, making such a mess of the kitchen. Then the contestant's fiddle bow, sliding across the strings with lightning speed, caught her attention. She stared at the fiddler on stage in complete amazement. "Incredible," she thought.

"And our last contestant..." Charlie announced.

"What?" Darcy looked at Jack.

"You ready?" he said.

"Oh, crap."

"...is Miss Darcy Marshall, all the way from Prestonsburg, Kentucky."

Darcy and Jack made the long walk from the waiting area past the lines of fans toward the stage. As she passed the fiddler who had just finished, they both raised their hands to consummate the traditional high-five, a sign of mutual respect and admiration. Darcy and Jack arrived on stage and took their place under the hanging microphone. Darcy looked over at Charlie and smiled. He winked at her as he announced the tunes she would be playing.

"Judges," Charlie said. "Darcy Marshall. She'll be playing *Tom and Jerry, Festival Waltz,* and *Don't Let the Deal Go Down.* Darcy Marshall."

The room was dark, except for the beams of light shining directly on them from the ceiling. Darcy paused for a moment, closed her eyes, and pointed her face toward one of the spotlights.

"Lord, thank you for bringing me here," she whispered to herself. "May it be your will."

She opened her eyes and nodded at Jack. He returned the nod. Her long red dress with the white ruffles on the shoulders and bottom was electrifying in the spotlights. It was just short enough to show the tops of her black cowgirl boots with sparkling trim.

Darcy struck two notes and led off into her required hoedown, *Tom and Jerry.* She quickly got the attention of the judges and the crowd. They were mesmerized. Her long blonde hair whipped left and right as she tapped her foot and swayed her hips to the beat of the tune. Her smile was so big, it pulled the whole audience right into the music with her.

When that tune was over, she paused for a few short seconds as the crowd tentatively applauded, then began playing *Festival Waltz.* She remembered playing it for Tracy as she lay in her cradle the day she brought her and Mary Alice home from the hospital. She closed her eyes and was there all alone—her, her fiddle, her music, and her memories. This waltz was for Tracy—her and God. On the last note, she opened her eyes and looked up again. She smiled with a tear on her cheek.

"You've got this. Go girl," Jack said softly, preparing her for the big finale.

Her tune of choice, *Don't Let the Deal Go Down.* "Make it fun," she quickly whispered back to him, then kicked off the tune with a rapid fire intro.

Jack jumped in with such a driving rhythm that she couldn't help but drive right along with him. Again, her hair was whipping from one side to the other, her smile lighting up the room. The crowd started clapping and stomping their feet to the beat of Jack's rhythm and Darcy's bow, streaking up and down on the strings, throwing rosin and broken horse hair in all directions.

Jack kept the tempo going strong, but then he started laughing softly to himself, like he couldn't believe he was actually part of this, an out-of-body experience, perhaps.

As soon as Darcy reached the end of the tune, she pelted the strings with the last few notes and Jack made his last G-run to the finish. Darcy thrust her fiddle in one hand and bow in the other, straight up in the air, barely missing the microphone hanging from above. The crowd jumped to their feet in a roar. The whistles and cheers were deafening in the gymnasium.

Darcy looked up the aisle between the seats and saw Judy laughing and clapping her hands at the back of the room. Standing to one side of Judy was Kevin. Then she looked to the other side. It was Ben, standing there with Rick. She squinted. She was confused. In front of Rick were Tracy Lynn and Alison.

"Oh, my God," she said. But nobody could hear her over the roar. Jack stood to the side and applauded for her, right along with the audience. Tears ran down Darcy's face as she pointed to the twins at the back of the gym with her bow.

When the crowd began to quiet down and Jack walked off the stage, Darcy turned to follow him but was distracted by an object in the corner of her eye. She looked over at the edge of the stage. It was Trevor, standing with his hands together over his mouth. He smiled with tears running down his face. Darcy froze.

In the back of the room, Alison tugged on Judy's shirt sleeve. "Aunt Judy. Look, it's Papaw." She pointed over to the side of the stage.

"Oh, my Lord," Judy said, looking at Rick. "Did you know he was coming?"

"Surprise to me," he said.

Kevin shrugged his shoulders.

Darcy started walking again and handed her fiddle to Jack. He took it, confused, but without saying a word. Darcy kept her bow and walked down the steps and off the stage, straight over to Trevor. Their eyes were locked. She held the bow in the open palms of her hands and stretched her arms out, as if surrendering it to him. He took it from her and wrapped his arms around her. Darcy sunk her face into Trevor's neck in a deep embrace, crying. Judy put her hands over her mouth, tears running down her cheeks. The crowd began applauding again.

Darcy didn't win that year. Not the fiddle contest, anyway. She won something much more dear to her. Her husband. Her granddaughters. Her friends. She came in second with the folks at Weiser. She loved her experience there and they learned who Darcy Marshall was. She would be back.

When Trevor and Darcy got back home, they were together. They unpacked and went straight into the music room.

"I sure have missed this place," Trevor said.

"This place has missed you," Darcy said, smiling across the room at him.

She told Trevor about what had happened in the tent the year before—the conversation with God. He told her of a similar conversation he too, had had with God that put him on a plane to Idaho.

"I went over and had a long talk with Preacher Stan last week, too," he said.

"You did?" Darcy asked, grinning.

"Yes. I've really missed you, honey, and being alone for so long gave me a lot of time to think. I told Stan I wanted to learn how to pray. He spoke to me about building my relationship with God and how important he thought that was to you...and to me."

"I...I'm speechless," she said.

"Do you mind if we call him up and see when I can get baptized? I want you to be with me."

Darcy got up from her chair in tears, and sat on his lap. "Of course I don't mind. Do you know how long I've prayed for this day?"

Darcy and Trevor went to Stan's church that Sunday morning, and Trevor was baptized. Darcy cried the whole time while Sue, Stan's wife, had an arm around Darcy. Rick and the twins were there too, along with the entire band. Everyone cheered and clapped when Trevor came out of the water.

After church, Trevor stopped to speak to Preacher Stan on his way out the door.

"Thanks, Stan. You've been a really big help to me and a blessing to this family. I think we'd like to start attending church here, if that's okay with you."

Stan looked at Darcy's big smile and shook Trevor's hand.

"Of course I don't mind. We'll see you next week!"

When they left, the whole family drove across town to visit the graves of Tracy and Dawn at the old church. They climbed out of the car and walked through the gate into the cemetery.

"You've kept it up real nice," Darcy said as she took Rick's arm.

"I miss her so much," he said.

"I know you do. She'd be really proud of how you're doing with these girls."

Tracy Lynn and Alison stood, not saying a word, looking at Dawn's headstone, and then at Tracy's.

Tracy Lynn started reading the inscription on the plaque that stood between the headstones.

Sisters

Today as I walk through this dream we call life,
I think of the one with the blister.
Though her gift is so big, she never forgets,
there is no tighter tie than a sister.

We dance and we sing, we share everything.
We fight, though the win so clearly with her.
She laughs and reminds me of her other family,
yet there's no tighter tie than a sister

She's one year older, my hero I'd say.
I'd do anything to assist her.
Her music so dear, and God is so near.
But there's no tighter tie than a sister.

She never lets others get in between us.
When smiling, no one can resist her.
I'm never alone in this world, 'cause you know,
There's no tighter tie than a sister."

Tracy Lynn and Alison both looked up at their Nana. "Your mom wrote that for your Aunt Tracy," Darcy said. "A long time ago."

Tracy Lynn, not saying a word, took Alison's hand in hers and they walked away. Darcy, Trevor, and Rick turned, smiling, as they watched the girls walk across the cemetery yard and into the shade of the big weeping willow.

APPENDIX A

The Peghead Solution

In our story, *Strings of Faith*, our main character, Darcy, discovered what I now refer to as **The Peghead Solution**. This solution is based on the four primary notes on her fiddle: E for Empathy, A for Attitude, D for Devotion, and G for Gratitude. These principles are essential for developing the Joy Made Full that Jesus prayed for in John 17:13 [NASB]. I am providing this appendix as a free workbook that might help you take a deep dive into your personal relationships, with the goal of establishing a solid foundation upon which to build them. Virtually every aspect of life requires strong relationships—yes, even for those of us who are introverts.

Below are some thought-provoking questions to help you reflect on your own life, like Darcy, to see how you're doing with the pegs of Empathy, Attitude, Devotion, and Gratitude. Tune each one of them, just as Darcy so carefully tuned her fiddle. If you would like more information about The Peghead Solution, or to contact the author about other aspects of his teachings, visit www.terrystafford.com.

I recommend that you include this book in your book club or Bible study group and use the below workbook as the basis for a 4-week study program. Enjoy!

EMPATHY

We have all experienced unfair judgment in our lives. Maybe we have been judged ourselves by someone in the church or the community for our shortcomings and character defects. If we think long and hard, we might even remember a time when we judged others harshly for the way they spoke, or dressed, or believed. This kind of judgment typically results from a lack of understanding, or stereotyping, or jumping to conclusions. Even engaging in hard-line interpretations of certain Bible passages can get us into trouble when looking at the lives of others, attempting to understand their motivations or belief systems.

1. Look up the definition of empathy. What does the word mean to you personally?

2. Can you think of a time when you weren't as empathetic toward another person as you should have been? Explain the circumstances.

3. How do you think you should have responded to the situation mentioned above?

4. If you are in a conversation with someone from a different faith background, how would you respond to a point of theological disagreement?

5. Explain how empathy helps us in our relationships:

ATTITUDE

We all have attitudes about our lives and our surroundings—pretty much everything we encounter. How we view the world and respond to it is a reflection of our attitude, driven by the paradigm or the glasses through which we view it. In fact, it is often said that nobody can hurt us beyond what we are willing to allow, based on our attitudes alone.

1. Look up the definition of attitude. What does the word mean to you personally?

2. How does your belief system or worldview affect your attitude?

3. Did your environment as a child have an impact on your attitude, either good or bad? Explain:

4. What are some of the ways you've been able to change your attitude about certain things?

5. Does attitude have an impact on your relationships? Explain:

DEVOTION

As we learned in Darcy's story, God plants the seed of a dream in each of us before we are even born. Then He entrusts us with gifts with which to pursue that dream. More often than not, we recognize this as children, but then are purged of it through social pressures or parental expectations. Our success or failure in reaching our dreams is directly proportional to our devotion to them—our ability to identify them and gain clarity around them. Once clarity is achieved, our devotion to a path is simplified. It's never too late.

1. Look up the definition of devotion. What does the word mean to you personally?

2. Besides your devotion to God and your family, do you have any dreams that you are devoted to? Explain:

3. Thinking back to your childhood, can you remember any gifts that God may have entrusted to you, in order to pursue a dream He planted? Had you forgotten about it? Why?

4. Do you have a dream for which you would like to gain clarity? A mission you know you should pursue? Explain:

5. This one might be a little more difficult. Does devotion in this context have an impact on your relationships? Explain:

GRATITUDE

We often go through life focused on our struggles and our pain. We stress over the obstacles to success and remain focused on some goal off in the future. When we become so goal-oriented, we fail to see the many blessings right in front of our face. It is important that we remain forever grateful for what God has already provided—and that we take time to pause and step away from our daily grind, to simply look around and be thankful.

1. Look up the definition of gratitude. What does the word mean to you personally?

2. Do you keep a gratitude journal or include daily gratitude in your life journal or planner? If so, how has it affected your attitude?

3. How are you at recognizing a kindness done for you, following it up with an outward show of gratitude? Give some examples:

4. Here are two verses from the Bible that refer to gratitude. Discuss how these verses apply to your life. Refer to your Bible for a more complete context.

Acts 24:3
Everywhere and in every way, most excellent Felix, we acknowledge this with profound **gratitude**.

Colossians 3:16
Let the message of Christ dwell among you richly as you teach and admonish one *another* with all wisdom through psalms,

hymns, and songs from the Spirit, singing to God with **gratitude** in your hearts.

5. Does gratitude have an impact on your relationships? Explain:

Notes:

Acknowledgements

I would like to thank God for getting me through this story so easily. Of course it was a lot of hard work putting things in some grammatically correct form, but the story itself poured out much easier than I had ever dreamed, once I sat and started writing. It only took me ten years to get to that point after the story showed up on my heart.

I would like to thank my wife, Gail, for putting up with my physical and emotional absence while writing this book.

My deepest gratitude goes to my sister, Sandra, and my niece, Julie, for their courage in sharing their story.

I would like to thank Cathy Yost and Eric Eaton, both Igniting Souls fellow tribe members whom I've never met in person, but have been such a blessing—Cathy, going above and beyond all of my expectations with her proofreading skills, and Eric, providing priceless recommendations to improve the story line.

I want to give a very special shout out to my editor, Precy Larkins, for her diligence and guidance, as well as all those who volunteered to proofread this work. Your input was priceless.

Finally, I want to thank my coach and mentor, Kary Oberbrunner, from the bottom of my heart. Without his guidance and encouragement, I may have been another ten years trying to get this story on paper. His wisdom and willingness to share his experience has been a true blessing. Thank you, sir.

Thank you all.
Terry

How to Connect

Connect with Terry on social media at:
www.terrystafford.com – *Joy Made Full* web site
@tlstafford on Twitter and Instagram
TerryStaffordAuthor on Facebook

Join the Strings of Faith Commnity

Get the backstory and a behind-the-scenes
look at *Strings of Faith*

Learn more about *The Peghead Solution*

Bring the story alive by actually listening to
the tunes that were mentioned

Sign up to Terry's email list for future offerings

www.StringsofFaithBook.com

About the Author

Terry Stafford

After spending most of his early life and years in the U.S. Navy searching for meaning, Terry is now on a mission to share what he has learned—in order to help people, find the *joy made full* that Jesus prayed for in John 17. He does this with the messages he delivers in his writing and speaking. He has been a worship leader for over fifteen years, leading the music ministry at his church, where he learned from everyone he came in contact with. For much longer than that, Terry has been playing bluegrass music with his wife and friends at shows and festivals around the country. In addition to being an author and project manager, he is a guitar player—but is beginning to accept himself as the self-taught fiddler that he is.

Terry holds an MA in Operations Management and is a certified Project Management Professional. He has been a Senior Project Manager with contractors at several NASA and DoD missile launch control centers around the country, and has taught business and project management courses in undergraduate programs at Embry-Riddle Aeronautical University.

Terry is a member of the American Christian Fiction Writers, and is active in the ranks of Author Academy Elite. His blogging and other writing includes inspirational topics for those who are seeking spiritual guidance—as well as for those who may have been hurt in some way by organized religion, and are looking for alternatives to traditional church, helping them to remain true to their faith, and engaged with their community.

Terry Stafford

When Terry isn't writing, speaking, and playing music—he loves spending time with his three grown children and numerous grandchildren, woodworking, and photography.

Bring Terry to your business or organization

Terry would love to speak to your group about
The Peghead Solution or other related
"Joy Made Full" inspirational topics

Terry understands the importance and the challenge of finding just the right speaker for an event—and that engaging the audience with a timely, relevant topic is essential. As a consultant, trainer, and ministry leader, he knows how the success of any event can easily hinge on the quality of the speaker.

Terry knows that equipping the audience with practical lessons and new perspectives on life's adventure, is critical to the impression they take out the door with them. He customizes each message or training package to achieve, and even exceed, the client's desired outcome.

Contact Terry today to check availability
or simply start the conversation

TerryStafford.com/speaking

CPSIA information can be obtained at www.ICGtesting.com
Printed in the USA
BVOW08*0937290916

463445BV00027B/38/P